Sports Illustrated KIDS

GRAPHIC NOVELS

STONE ARCH BOOKS
a capstone imprint

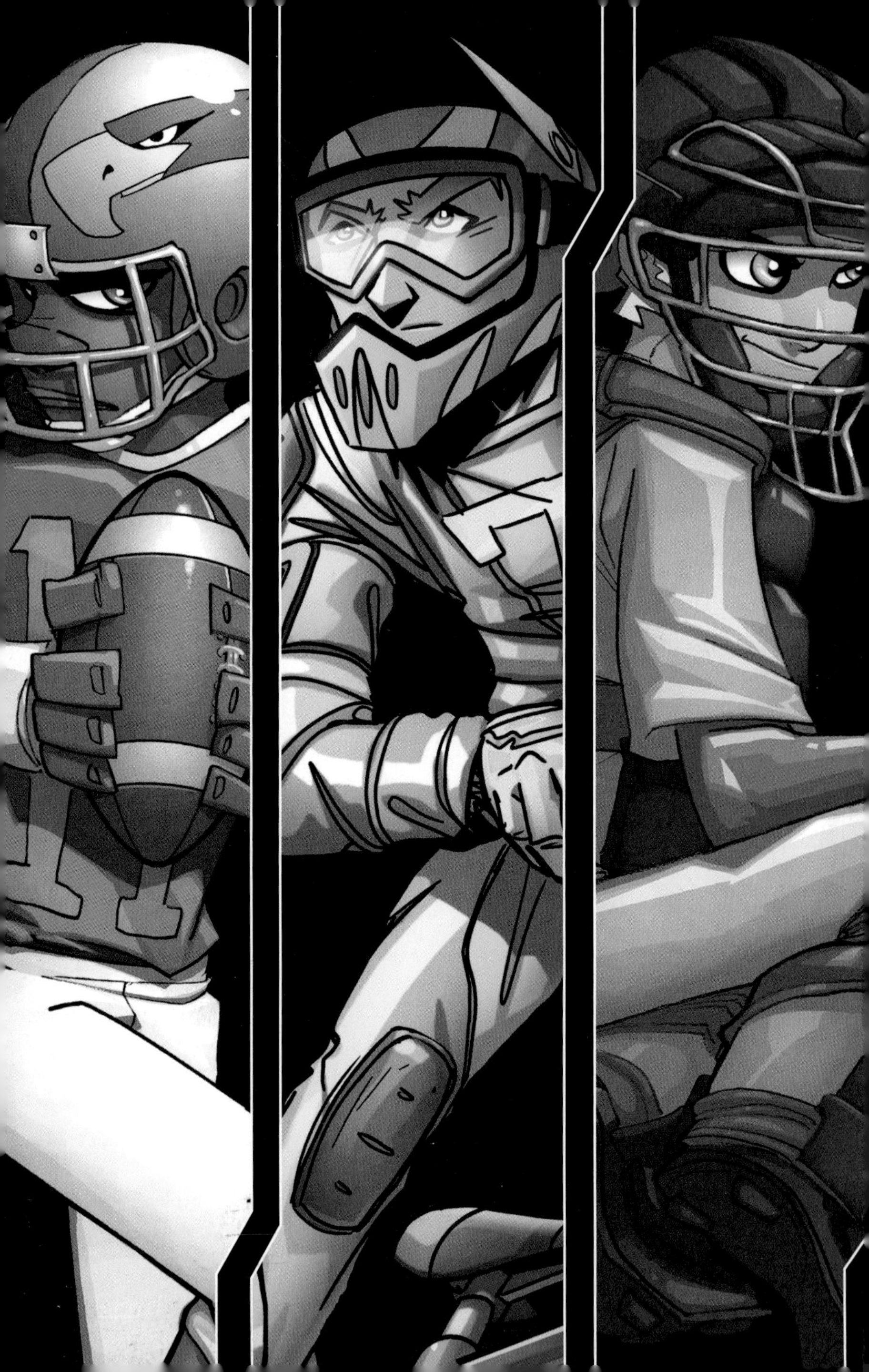

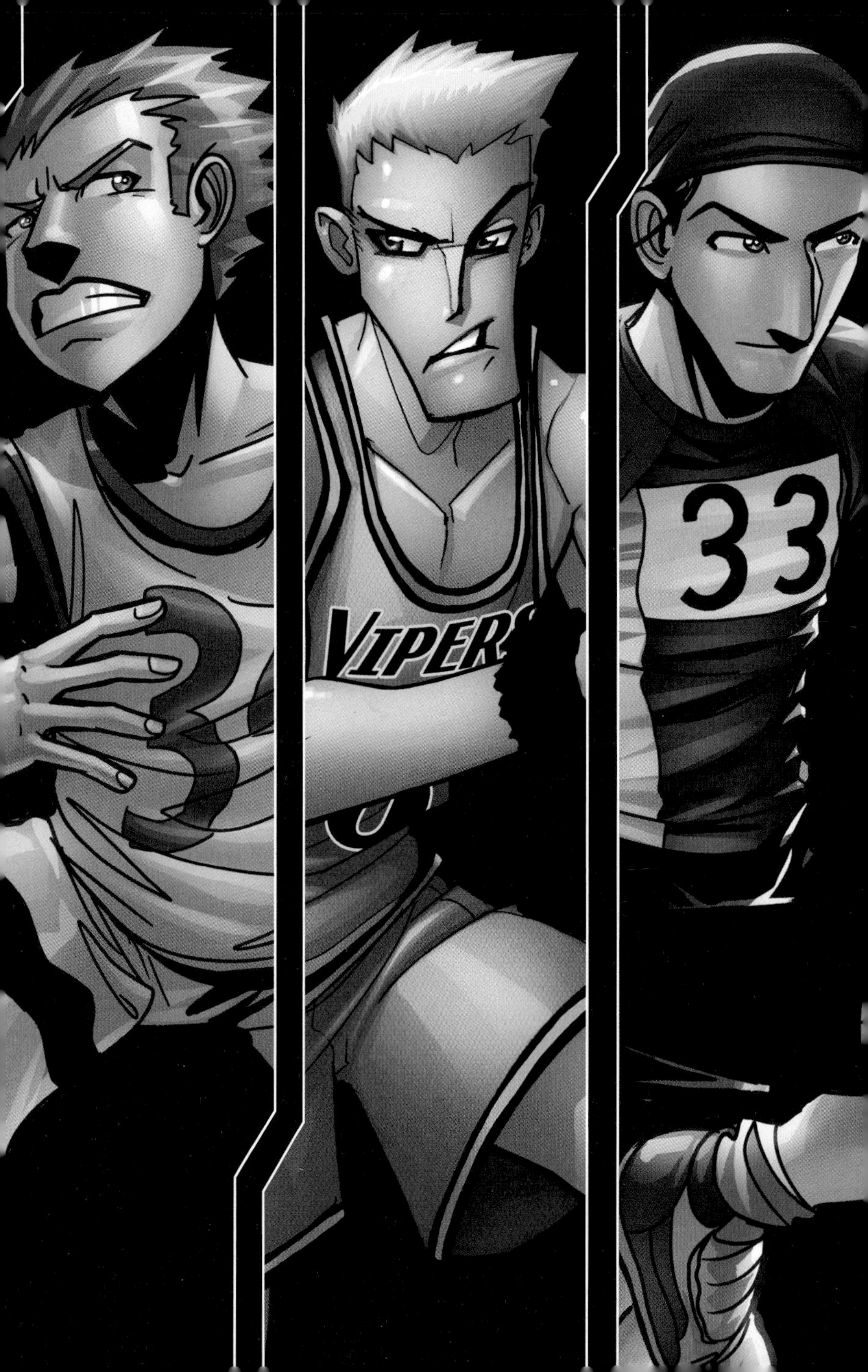
VIPERS
33

# UP NEXT ›››

on Sports Illustrated KIDS

:02 SPORTS ZONE SPECIAL REPORT

:04 FEATURE PRESENTATION:

# WILD PITCH

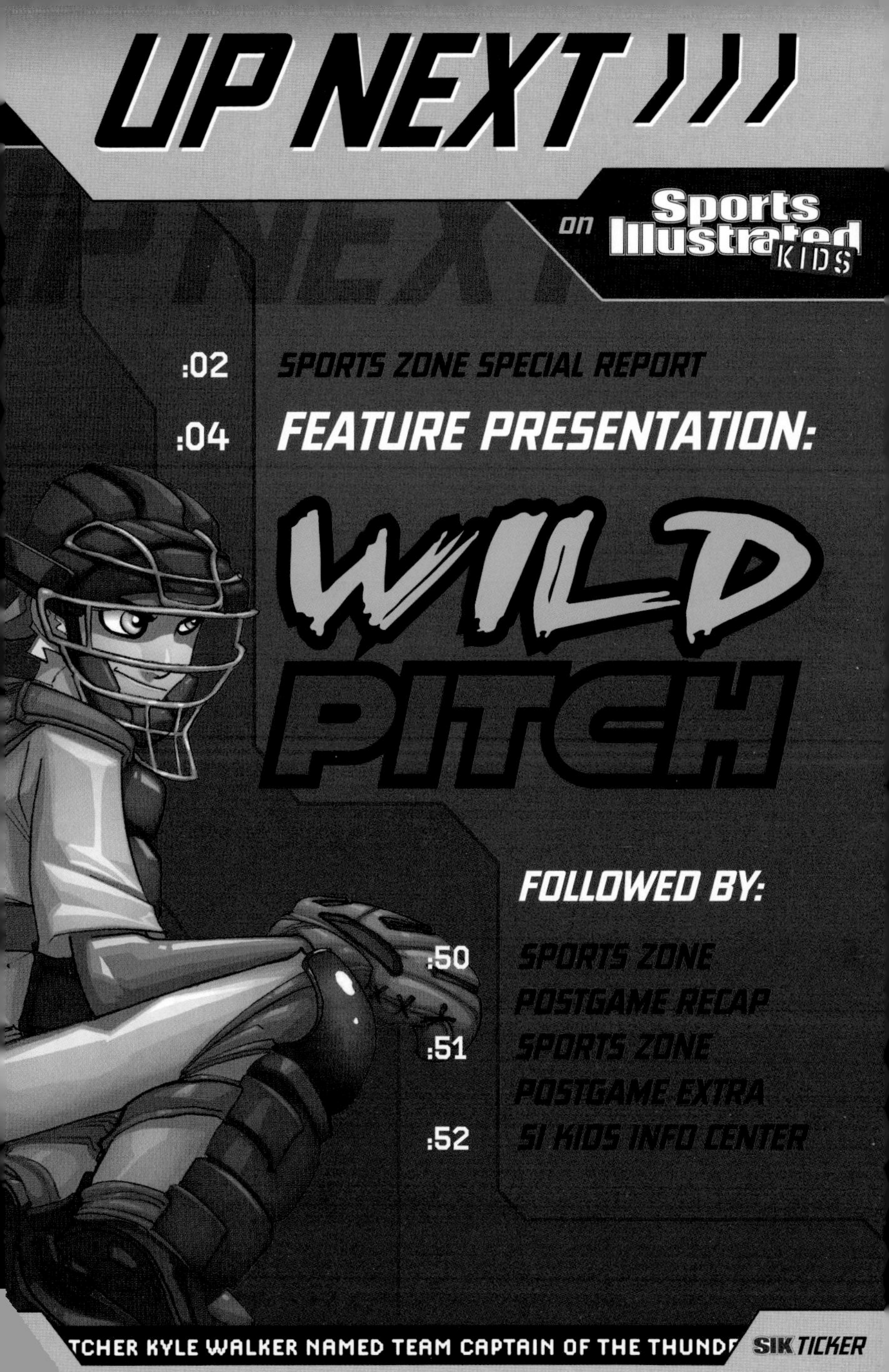

FOLLOWED BY:

:50 SPORTS ZONE POSTGAME RECAP

:51 SPORTS ZONE POSTGAME EXTRA

:52 SI KIDS INFO CENTER

TCHER KYLE WALKER NAMED TEAM CAPTAIN OF THE THUND

SIK TICKER

# SPORTS ZONE
## SPECIAL REPORT

**BSL**
BASEBALL

**PNT**
PAINTBALL

**FBL**
FOOTBALL

**SOC**
SOCCER

**BBL**
BASKETBALL

HKY

## NEW THUNDER PITCHER HAS TEAM CAPTAIN NERVOUS

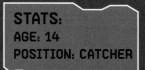

# KYLE **WALKER**

**STATS:**
AGE: 14
POSITION: CATCHER

**BIO:** Thunder team captain Kyle Walker is starting to worry about the team's newest pitching prospect, Ryan Rogan. Ryan relies mostly on his fastball, and opposing teams are starting to catch on. When Kyle tries to get Ryan to mix up his pitches a bit, Rogan refuses, and starts ignoring Kyle's pitch calls. Kyle just can't figure out why Ryan won't throw in a curveball once in a while ...

**Sports Illustrated KID$**

**UP NEXT:** WILD PITCH

BLZ vs BKS 3-1
TGR vs RDR 33-32
EAG vs BAN 14-7
SPA vs WLD 4-3
BAN vs RDR 21-15
RZR vs LIG 4-3
BLZ vs BKS 3-1

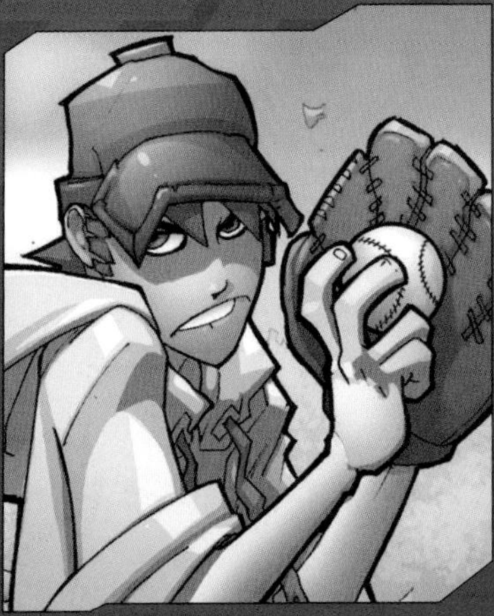

## RYAN ROGAN

**AGE:** 14
**POSITION:** PITCHER

**BIO:** Ryan's fastball is nearly impossible to hit — until he starts throwing it over and over and over . . . If Rogan would just learn to be a little less predictable with his pitches, he'd be every batter's worst nightmare.

## COACH CAMPOS

**AGE:** 44 **TEAM:** THUNDER

**BIO:** Coach Campos has little time for petty fights — he expects his athletes to stay focused and make teamwork top priority.

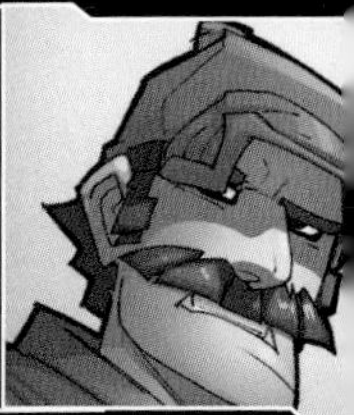

COACH

## MEGAN ROGAN

**AGE:** 7

**BIO:** Megan is Ryan's younger sister. She loves tea parties, her doll named Dolly, and getting really angry when she doesn't get her way.

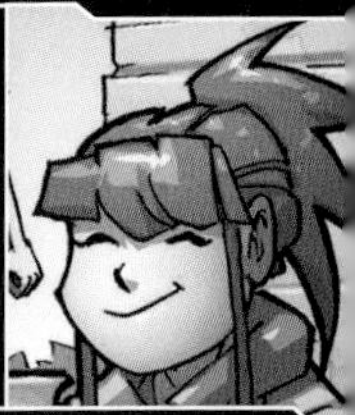

MEGAN

## GRANDPA WALKER

**AGE:** 76

**BIO:** Kyle Walker's grandfather listens well and loves to give Kyle some good old-man advice.

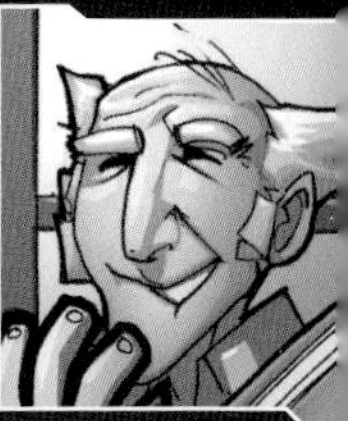

GRANDPA

RYAN ROGAN FORCED TO JOIN THUNDER FOR THIS SEAS

SIK TICKER

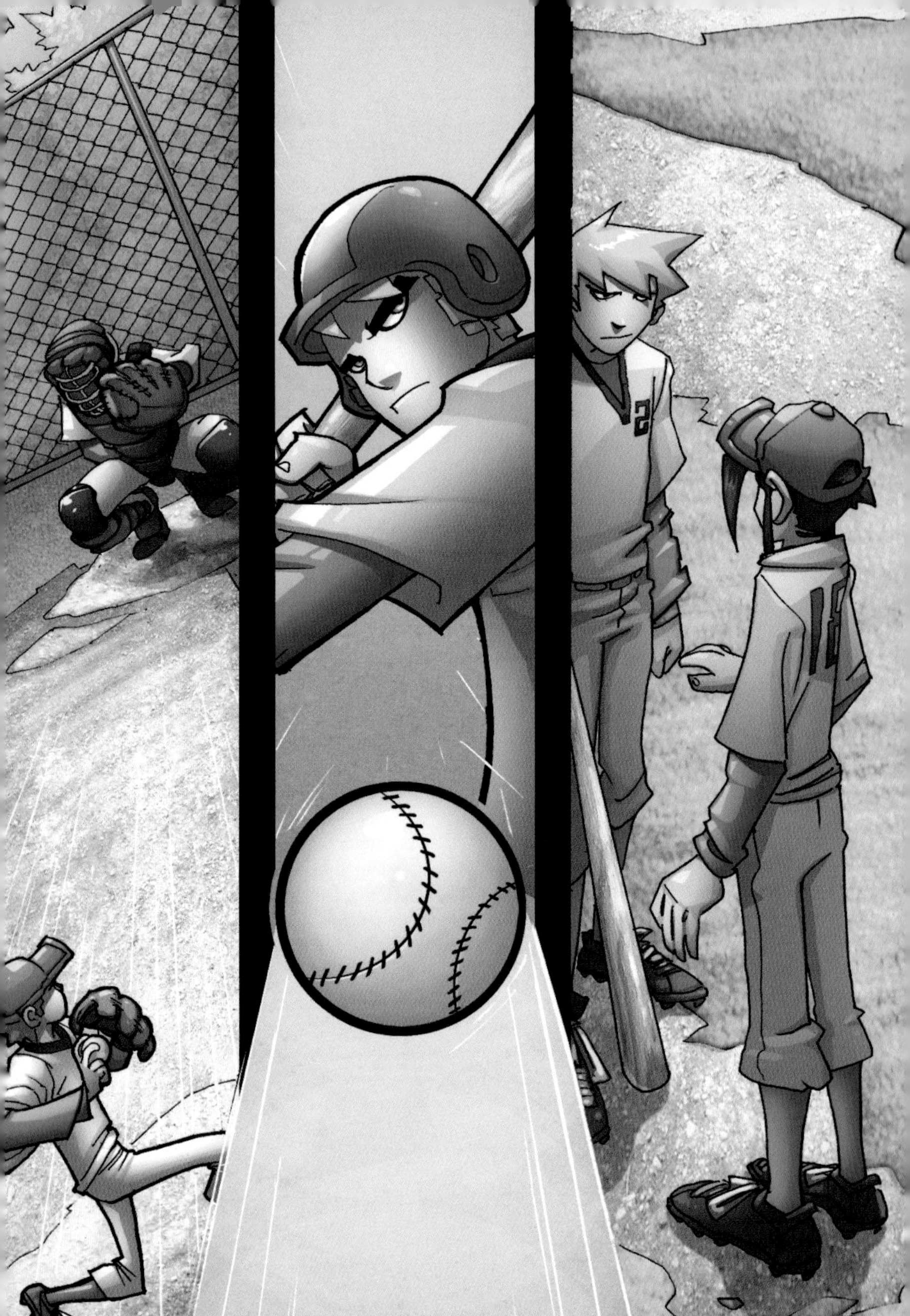

STAR CATCHER KYLE WALKER READY FOR FRESH START AFTER EXITING LAST

Sports Illustrated KIDS

PRESENTS

# WILD PITCH

A PRODUCTION OF

STONE ARCH BOOKS
a capstone imprint


written by Eric Fein
illustrated by Gerardo Sandoval
colored by Benny Fuentes

designed and directed by Bob Lentz
edited by Sean Tulien
creative direction by Heather Kindseth
editorial management by Donald Lemke
editorial direction by Michael Dahl



Sports Illustrated KIDS *Wild Pitch* is published by Stone Arch Books,
1710 Roe Crest Drive, North Mankato, Minnesota 56003.
www.capstonepub.com





Printed in the United States of America in North Mankato,
Minnesota.. 102015 009270R



Summary: In last year's state championship game, Ryan Rogan beaned Kyle Walker with a red-hot fastball. The pitch injured Kyle, forcing him to leave the game. His team lost, and it took several months for Kyle's injury to heal. He is certain that Ryan threw at him intentionally, but Kyle has put all that out of his mind, because he's excited for a fresh start this year — that is, until Ryan joins his team . . .



Library of Congress Cataloging-in-Publication Data
Fein, Eric.
Wild pitch / written by Eric Fein ; illustrated by Gerardo Sandoval and Benny Fuentes.
p. cm. -- (Sports Illustrated kids graphic novels)
ISBN 978-1-4342-2221-3 (library binding)
ISBN 978-1-4342-3073-7 (paperback)
ISBN 978-1-4342-4963-0 (e-book)
1. Graphic novels. [1. Graphic novels. 2. Baseball--Fiction.] I. Sandoval, Gerardo, ill. II. Fuentes, Benny, ill. III. Title.
PZ7.7.F45Wi 2011
741.5'973--dc22 2010032923


N'S PLAYOFFS BECAUSE OF A WILD PITCH THROWN BY RYAN ROGAN SIK TICKER

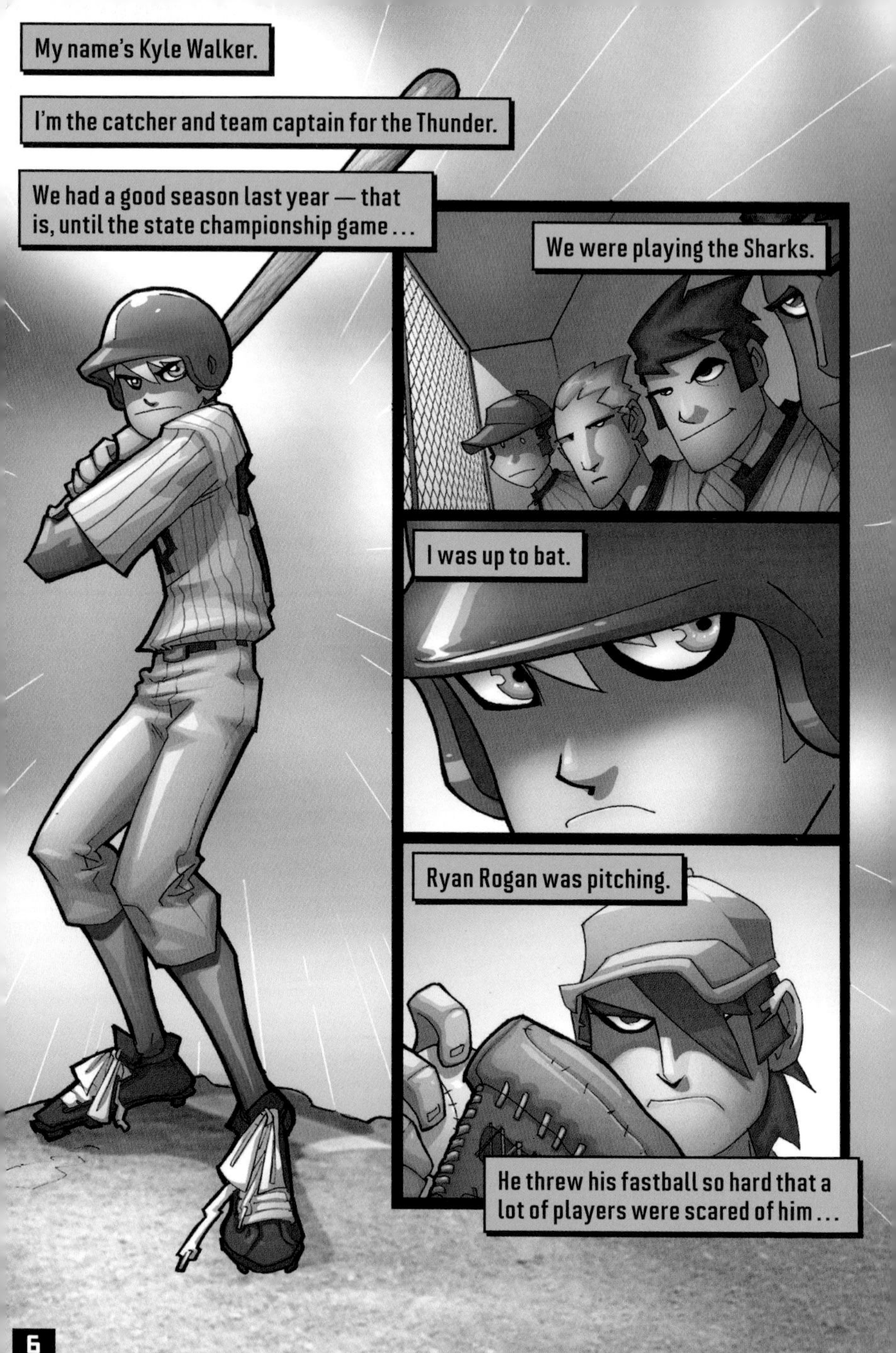
My name's Kyle Walker.
I'm the catcher and team captain for the Thunder.
We had a good season last year — that is, until the state championship game . . .
We were playing the Sharks.
I was up to bat.
Ryan Rogan was pitching.
He threw his fastball so hard that a lot of players were scared of him . . .

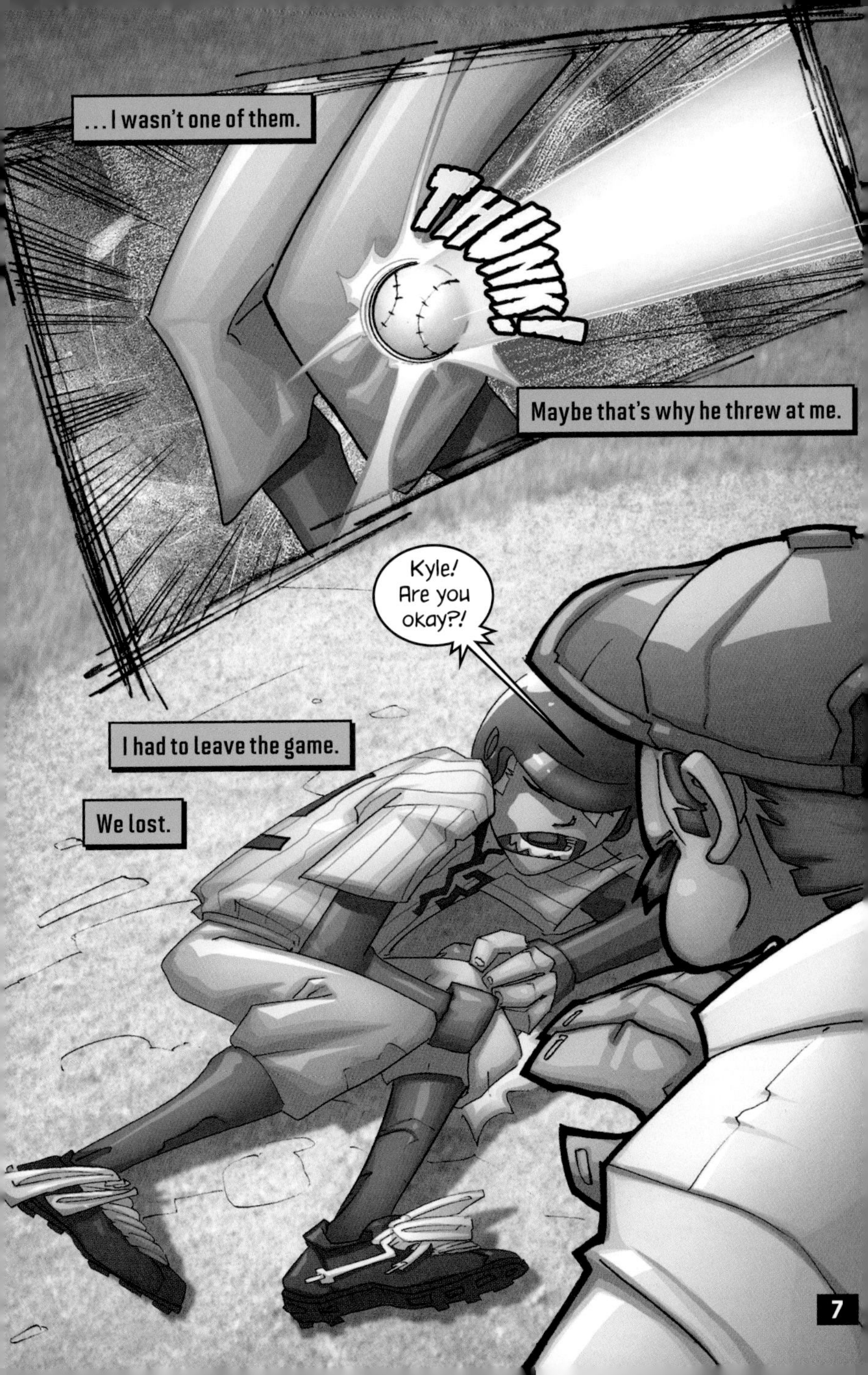
. . . I wasn't one of them.
THUNK!
Maybe that's why he threw at me.
Kyle! Are you okay?!
I had to leave the game.
We lost.

But that was last season. This year, I was looking forward to a fresh start.

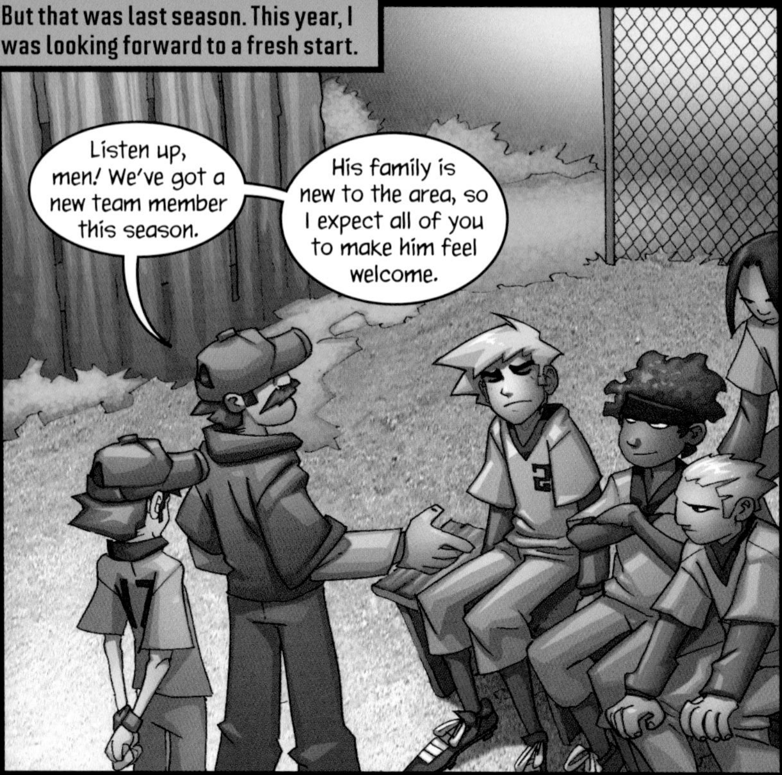
Listen up, men! We've got a new team member this season.
His family is new to the area, so I expect all of you to make him feel welcome.

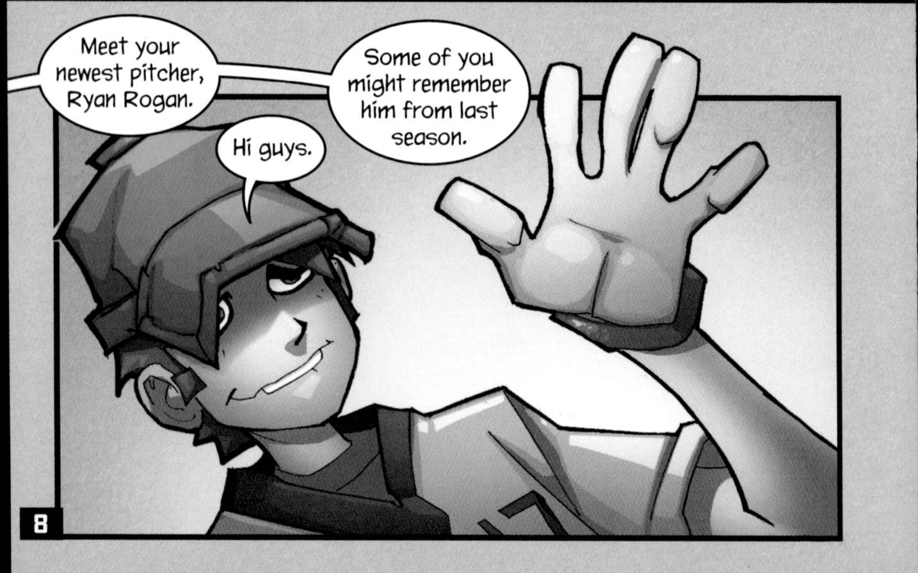
Meet your newest pitcher, Ryan Rogan.
Some of you might remember him from last season.
Hi guys.

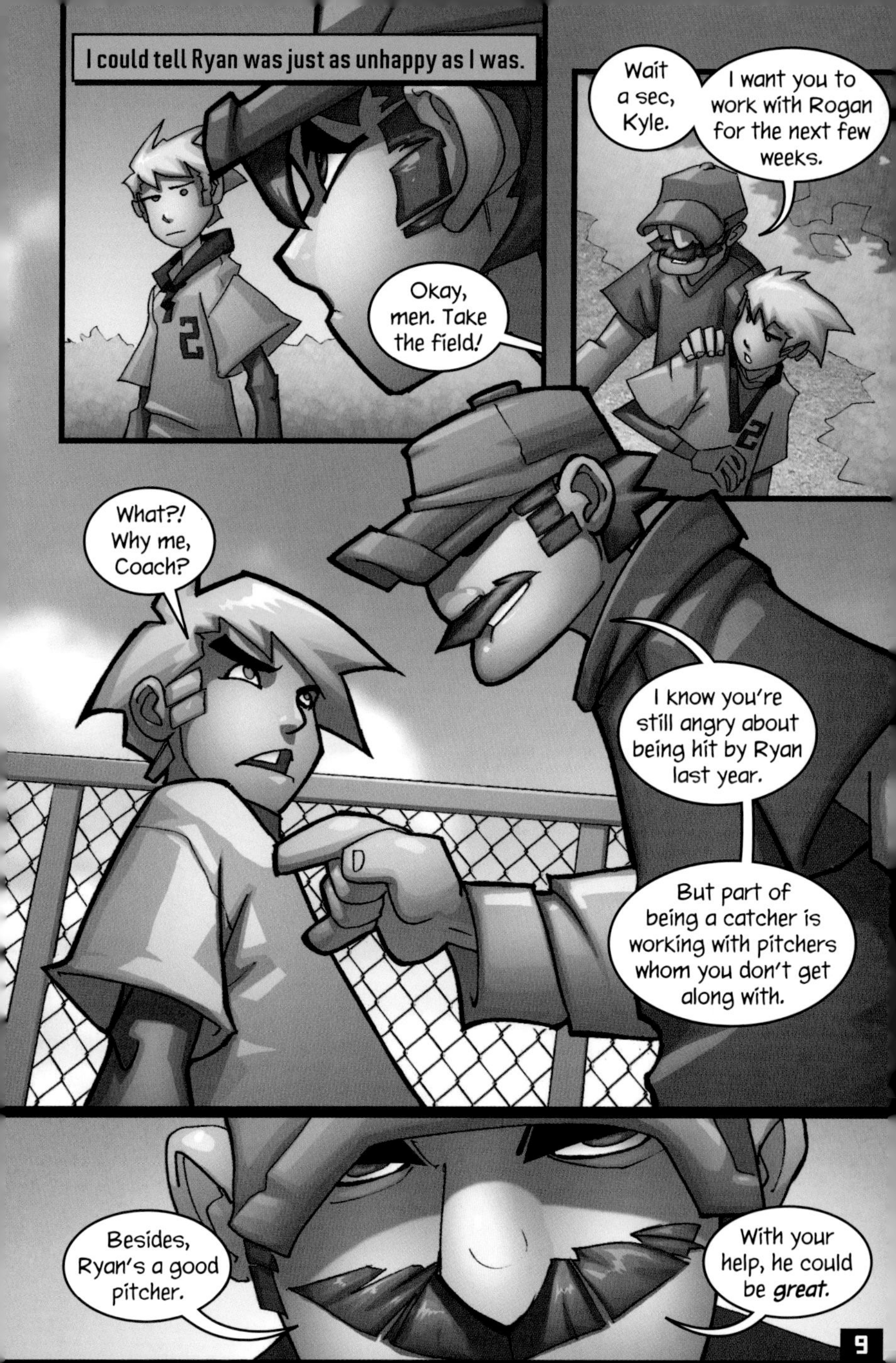
I could tell Ryan was just as unhappy as I was.
Okay, men. Take the field!
Wait a sec, Kyle.
I want you to work with Rogan for the next few weeks.
What?! Why me, Coach?
I know you're still angry about being hit by Ryan last year.
But part of being a catcher is working with pitchers whom you don't get along with.
Besides, Ryan's a good pitcher.
With your help, he could be *great*.

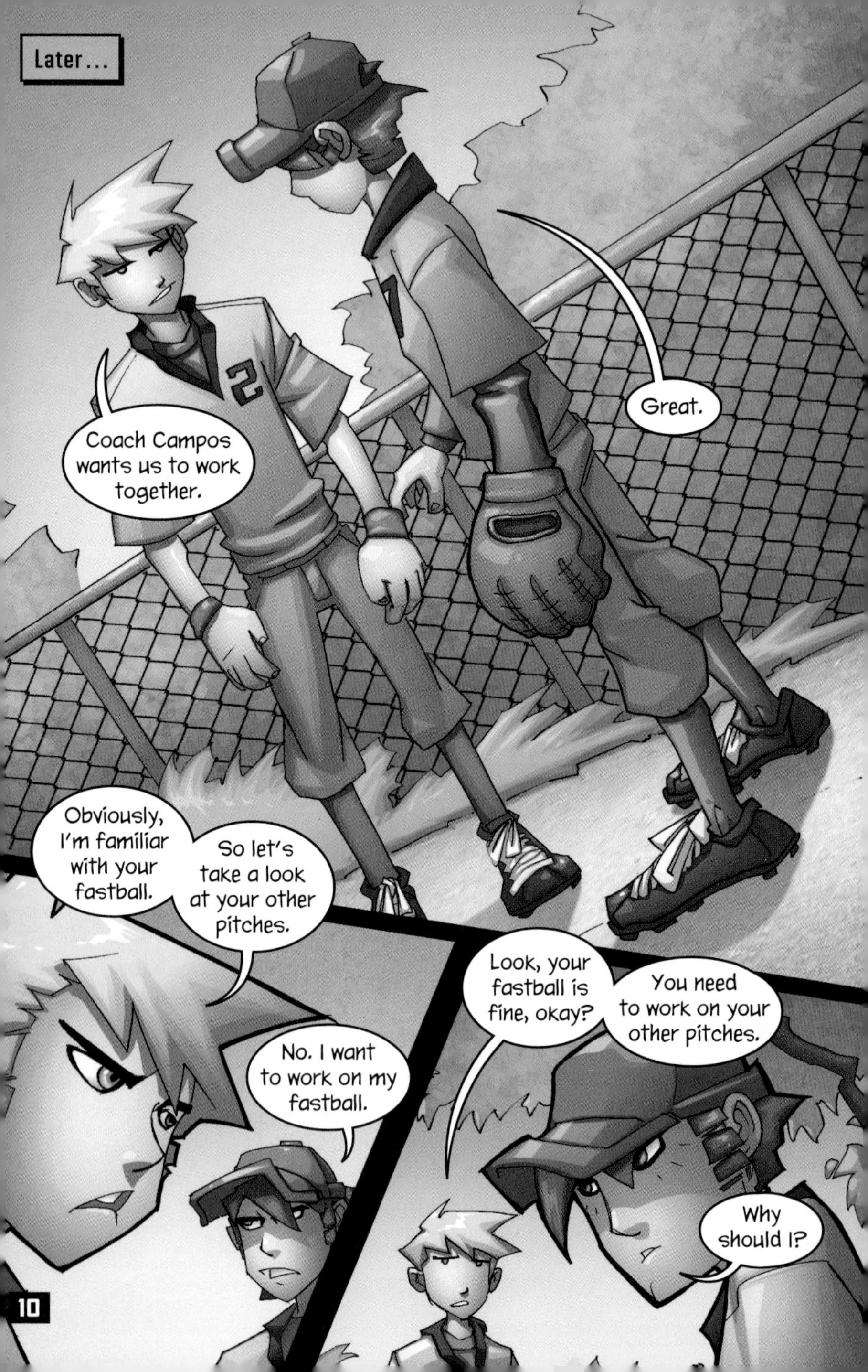
Later . . .
Great.
Coach Campos wants us to work together.
Obviously, I'm familiar with your fastball.
So let's take a look at your other pitches.
No. I want to work on my fastball.
Look, your fastball is fine, okay?
You need to work on your other pitches.
Why should I?

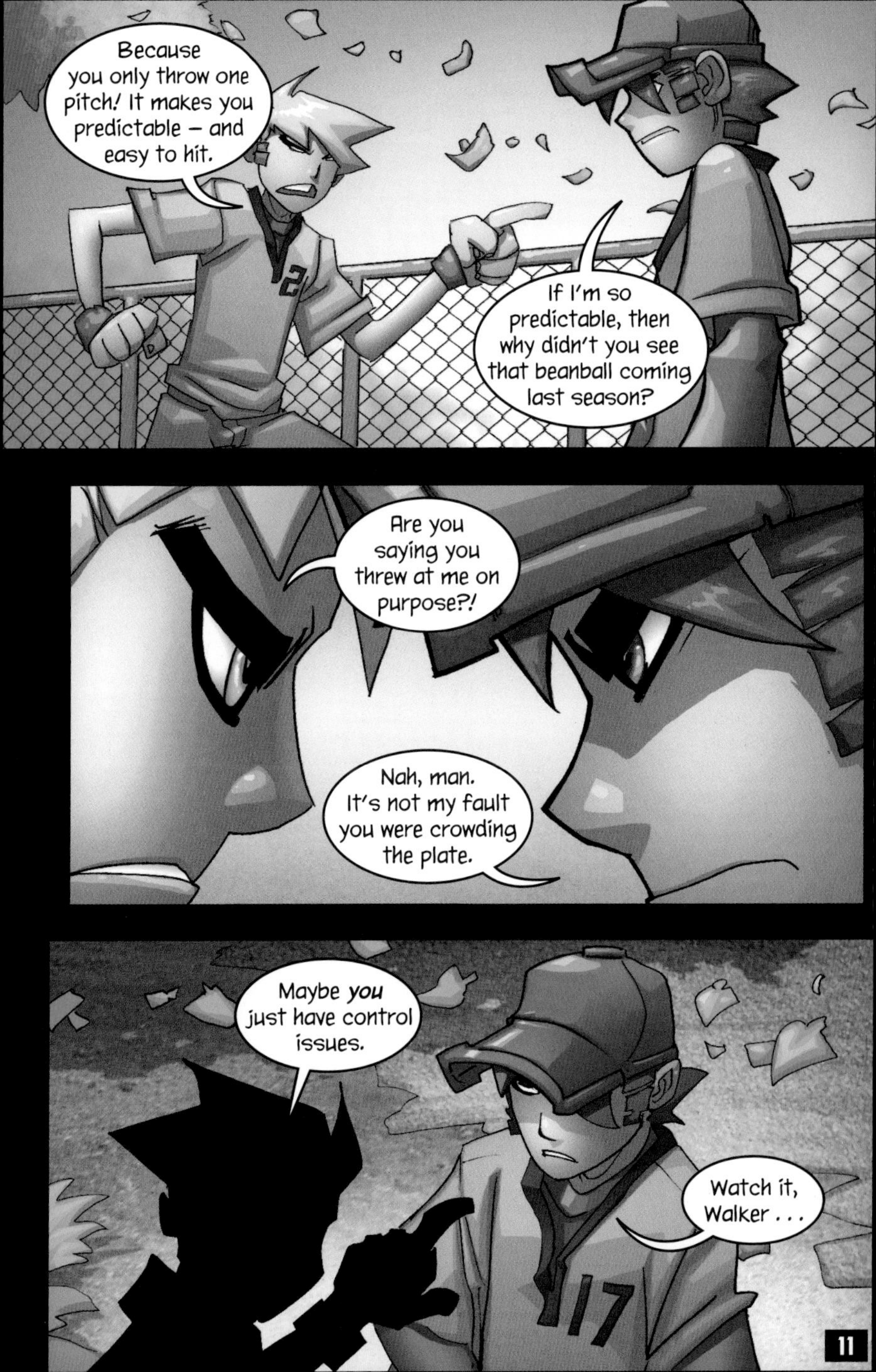
Because you only throw one pitch! It makes you predictable – and easy to hit.
If I'm so predictable, then why didn't you see that beanball coming last season?
Are you saying you threw at me on purpose?!
Nah, man. It's not my fault you were crowding the plate.
Maybe *you* just have control issues.
Watch it, Walker . . .

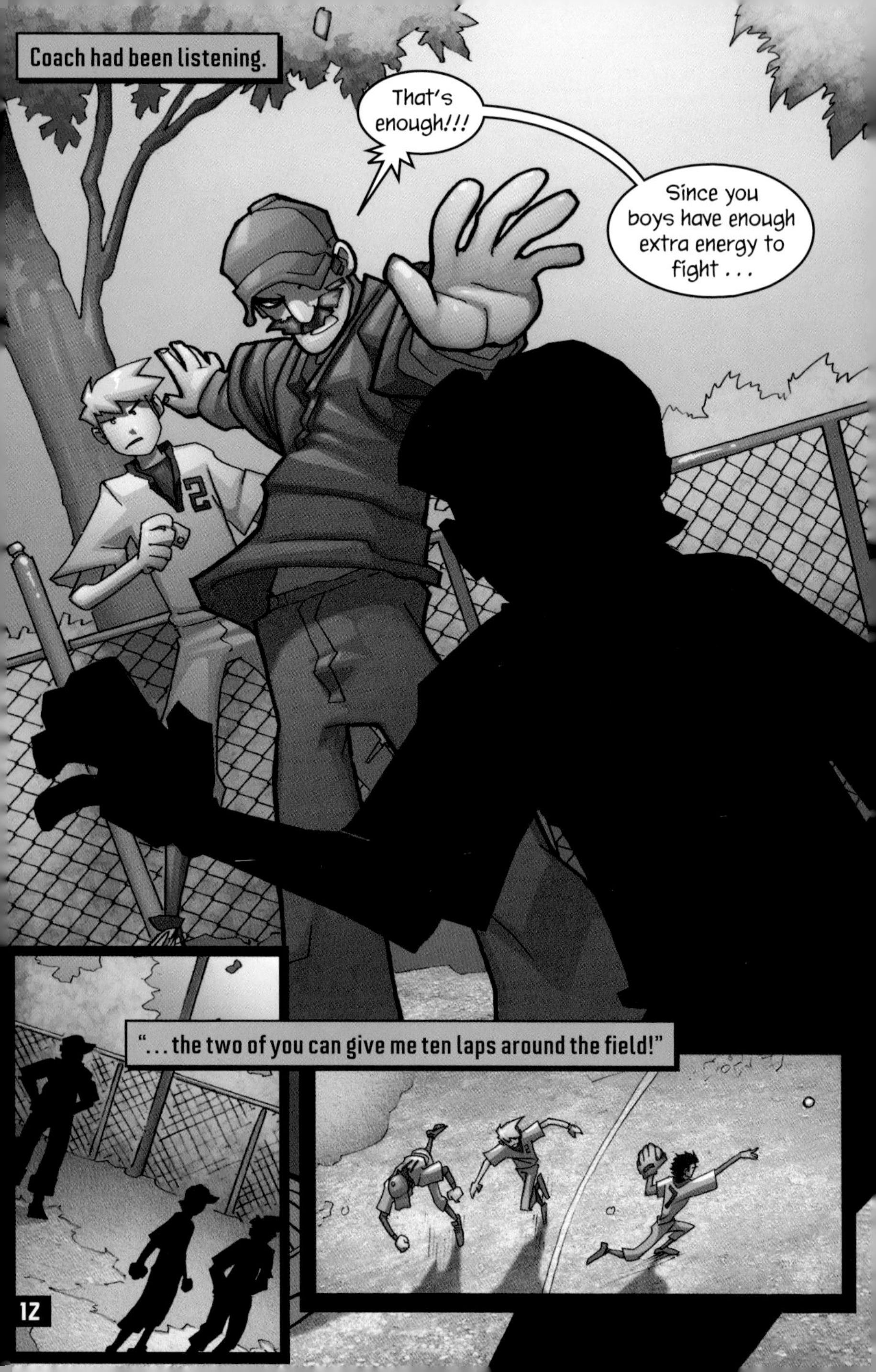
Coach had been listening.
That's enough!!!
Since you boys have enough extra energy to fight . . .
". . . the two of you can give me ten laps around the field!"

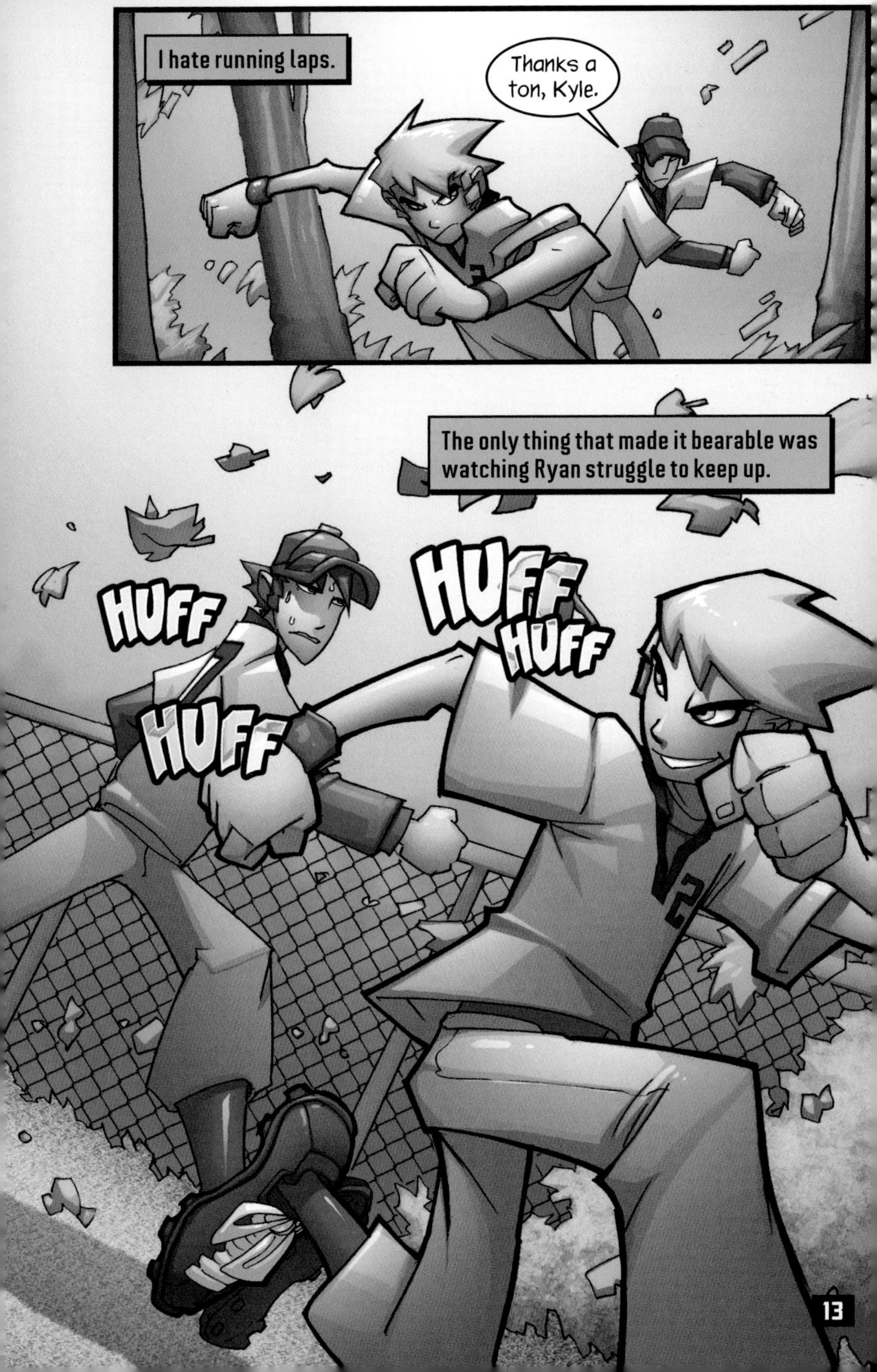
I hate running laps.
Thanks a ton, Kyle.
The only thing that made it bearable was watching Ryan struggle to keep up.
HUFF
HUFF
HUFF
HUFF

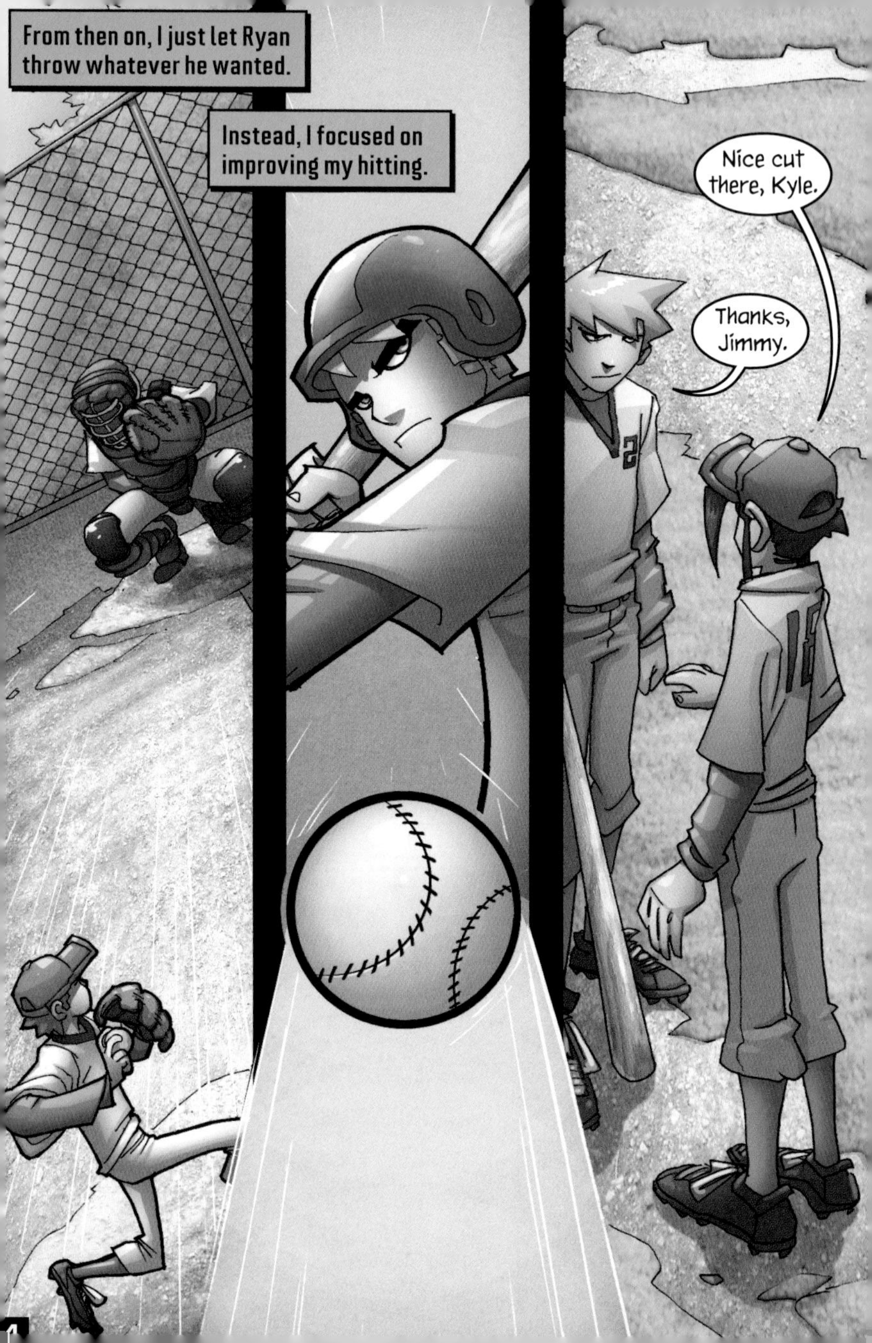
From then on, I just let Ryan throw whatever he wanted.
Instead, I focused on improving my hitting.
Nice cut there, Kyle.
Thanks, Jimmy.

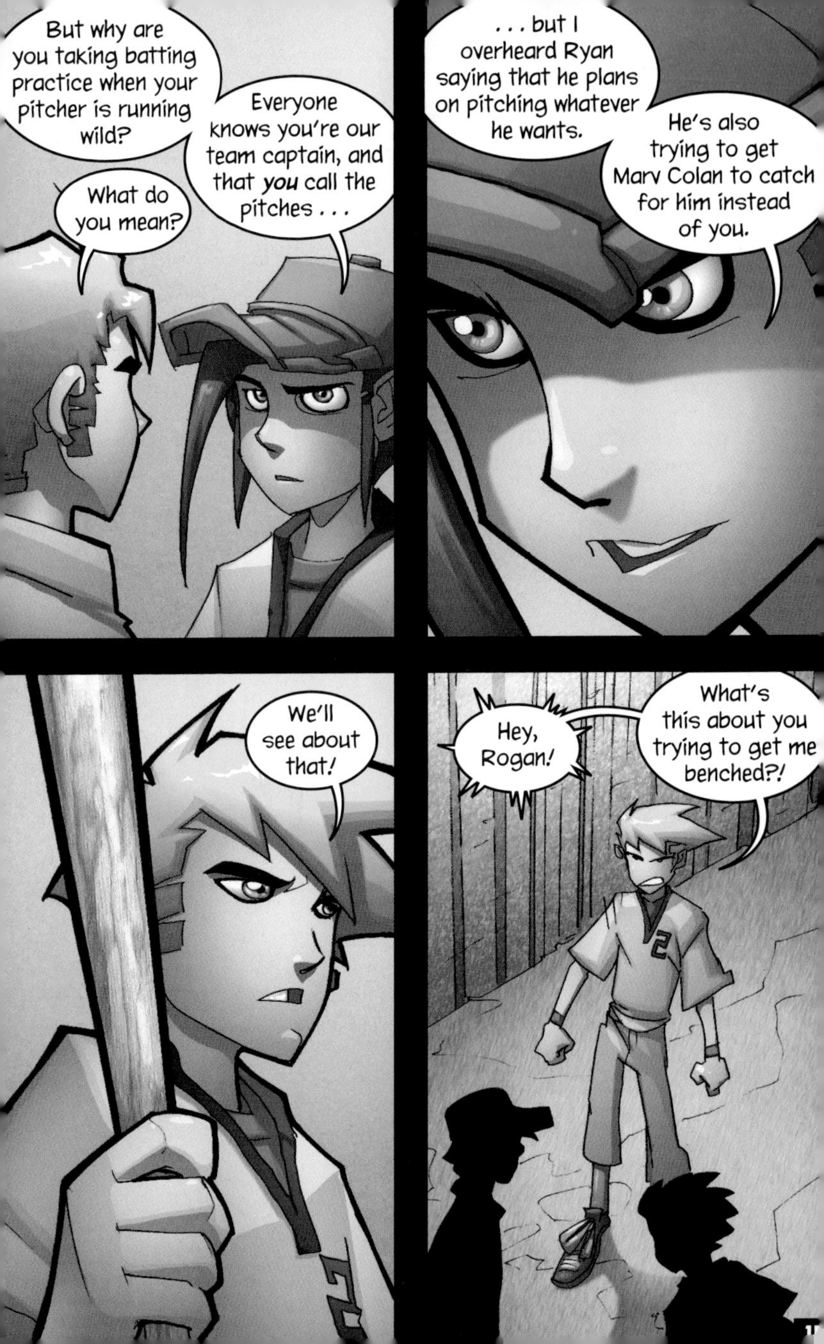
But why are you taking batting practice when your pitcher is running wild?
What do you mean?
Everyone knows you're our team captain, and that *you* call the pitches . . .
. . . but I overheard Ryan saying that he plans on pitching whatever he wants.
He's also trying to get Marv Colan to catch for him instead of you.
We'll see about that!
Hey, Rogan!
What's this about you trying to get me benched?!

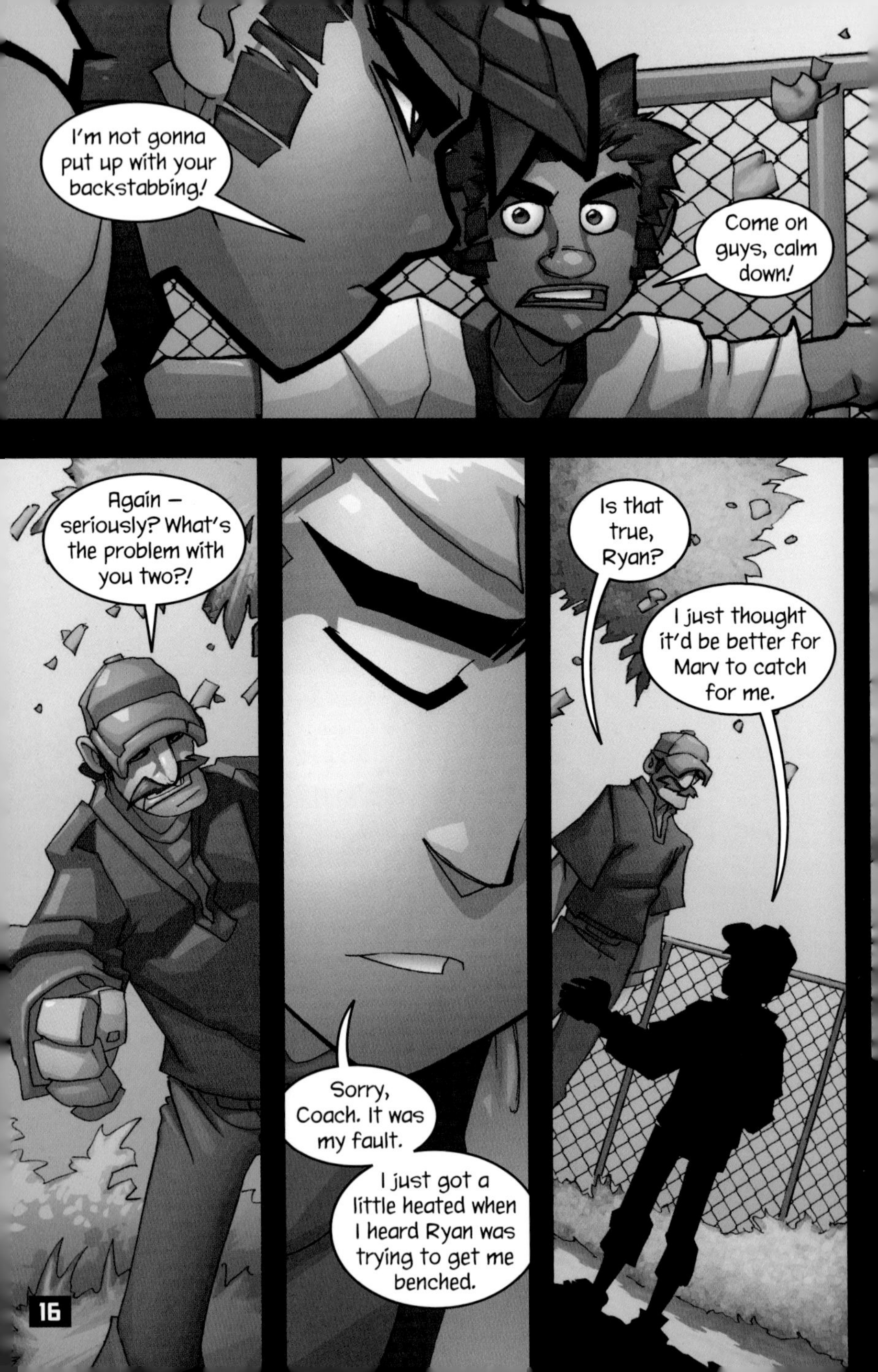
I'm not gonna put up with your backstabbing!
Come on guys, calm down!
Again – seriously? What's the problem with you two?!
Sorry, Coach. It was my fault.
I just got a little heated when I heard Ryan was trying to get me benched.
Is that true, Ryan?
I just thought it'd be better for Marv to catch for me.

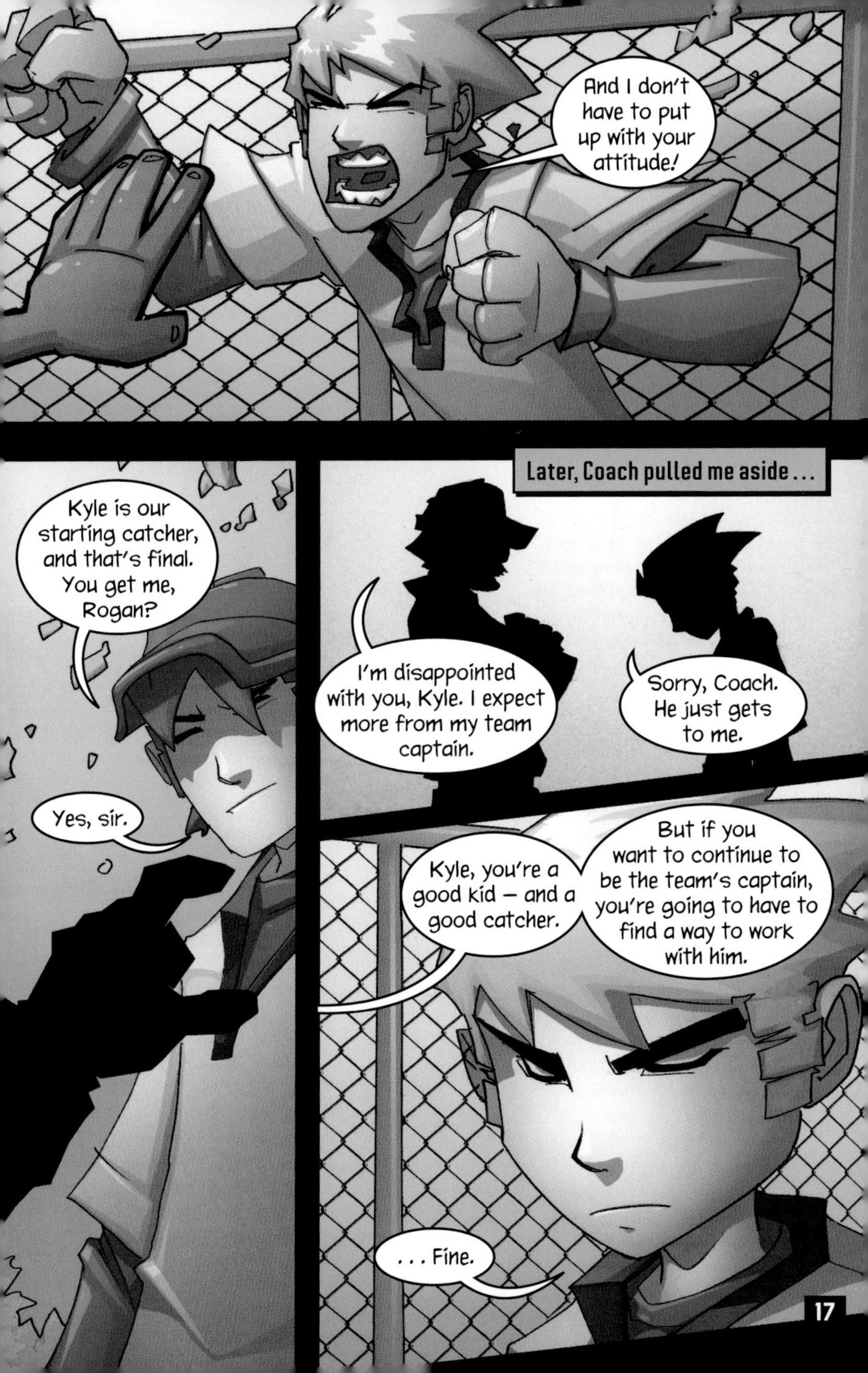
And I don't have to put up with your attitude!
Kyle is our starting catcher, and that's final. You get me, Rogan?
Yes, sir.
Later, Coach pulled me aside . . .
I'm disappointed with you, Kyle. I expect more from my team captain.
Sorry, Coach. He just gets to me.
Kyle, you're a good kid — and a good catcher.
But if you want to continue to be the team's captain, you're going to have to find a way to work with him.
. . . Fine.

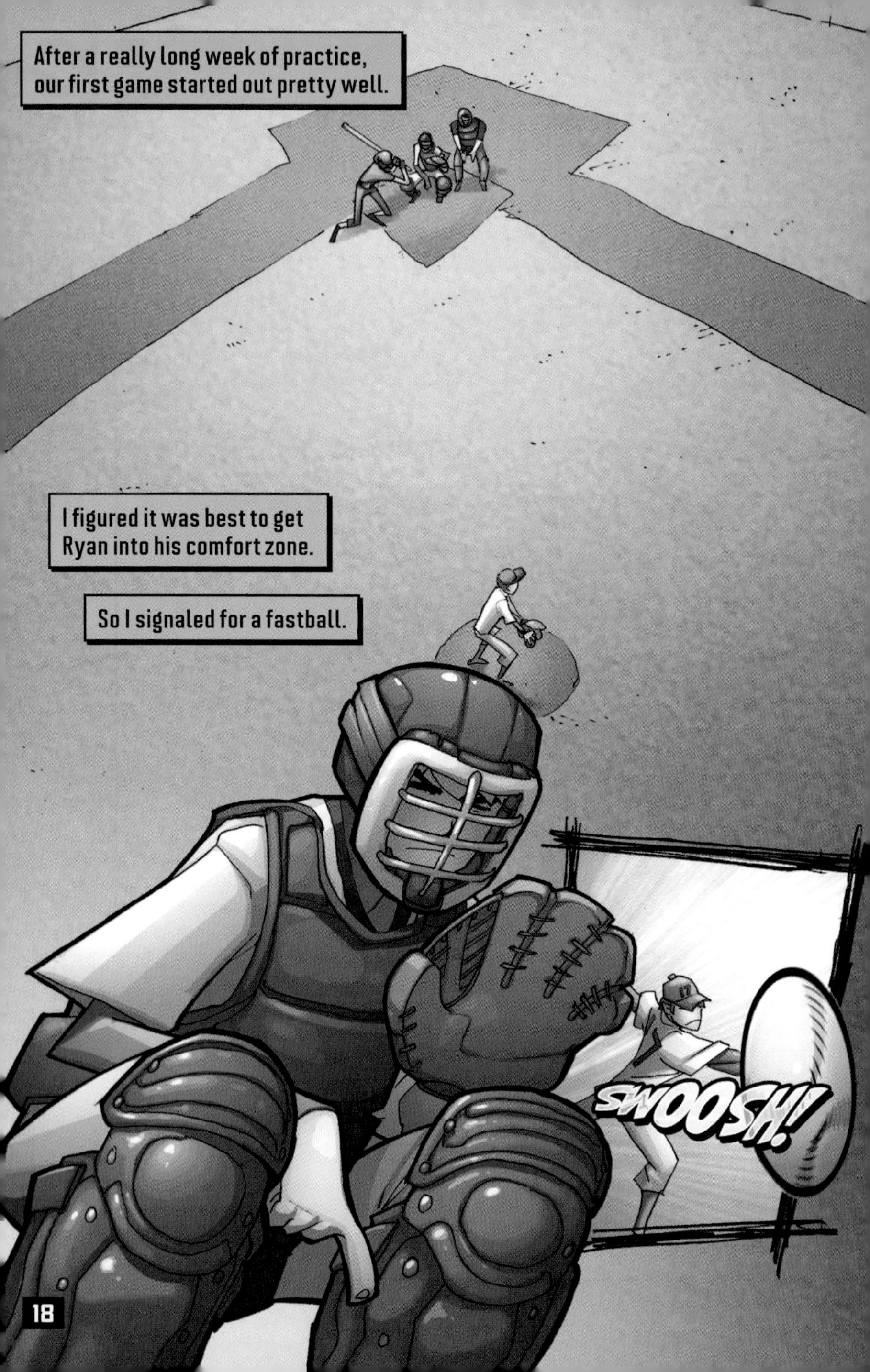
After a really long week of practice, our first game started out pretty well.
I figured it was best to get Ryan into his comfort zone.
So I signaled for a fastball.
SWOOSH!

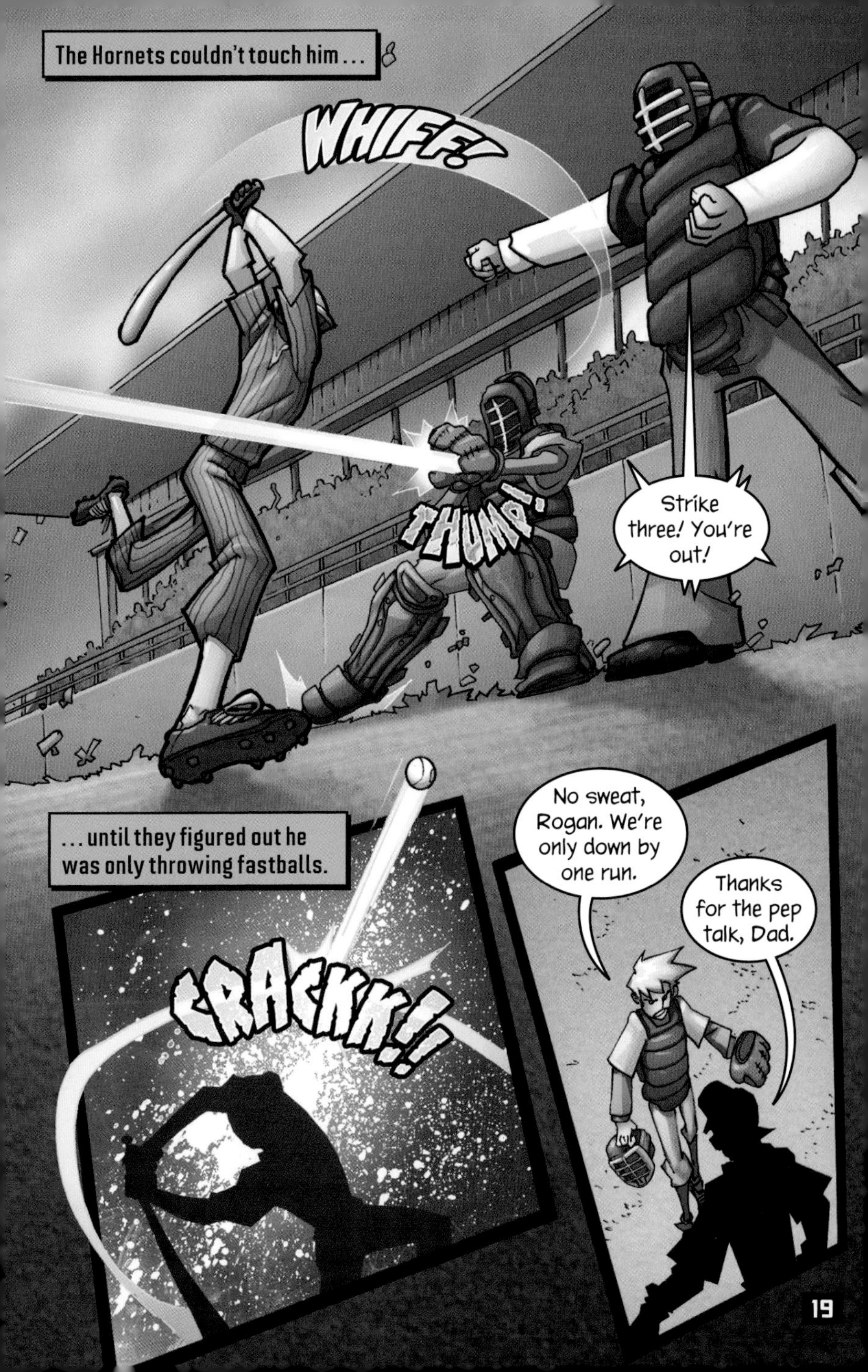
The Hornets couldn't touch him . . .
WHIFF!
THUMP!
Strike three! You're out!
. . . until they figured out he was only throwing fastballs.
CRACKK!!
No sweat, Rogan. We're only down by one run.
Thanks for the pep talk, Dad.

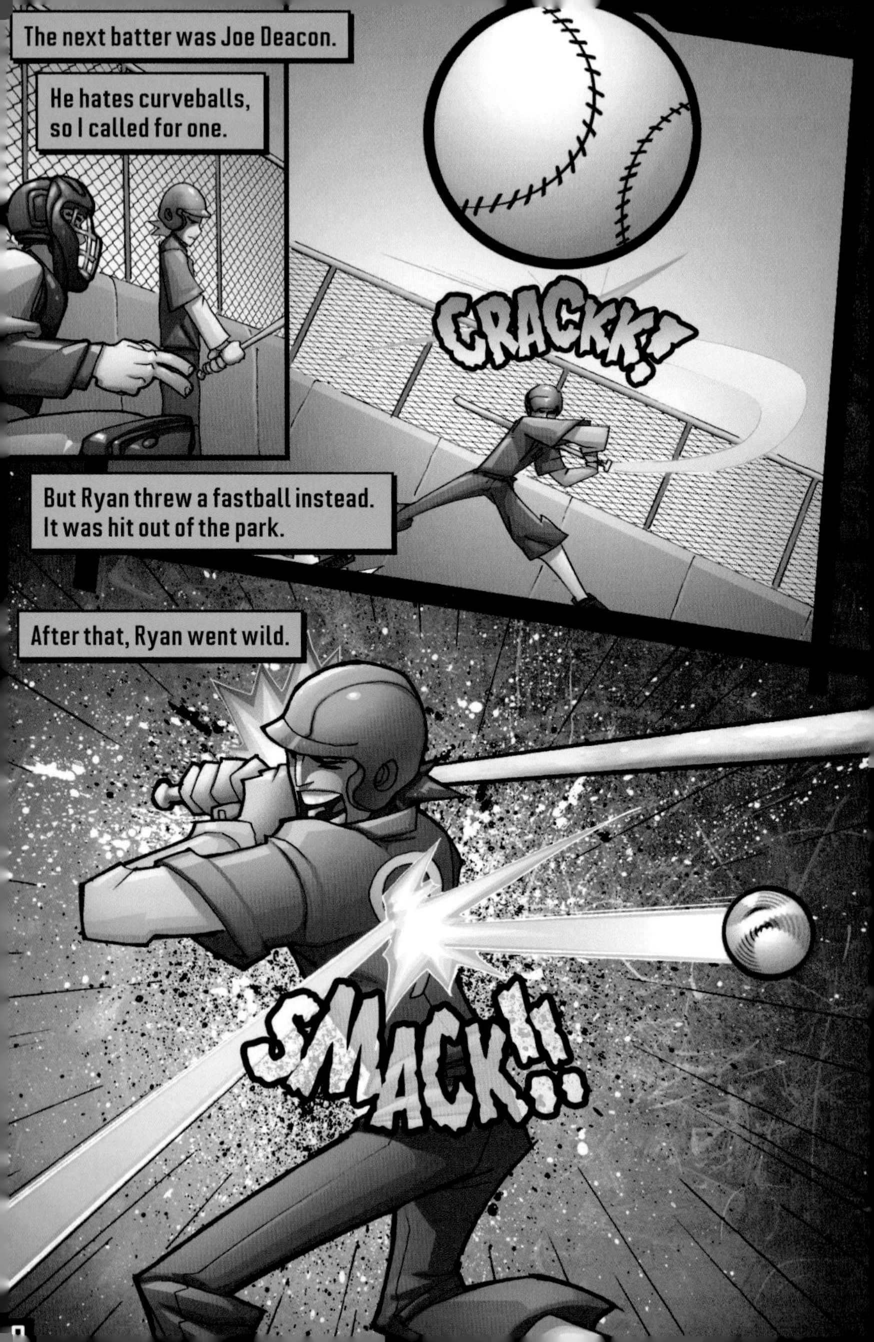
The next batter was Joe Deacon.
He hates curveballs, so I called for one.
CRACKK!
But Ryan threw a fastball instead. It was hit out of the park.
After that, Ryan went wild.
SMACK!!

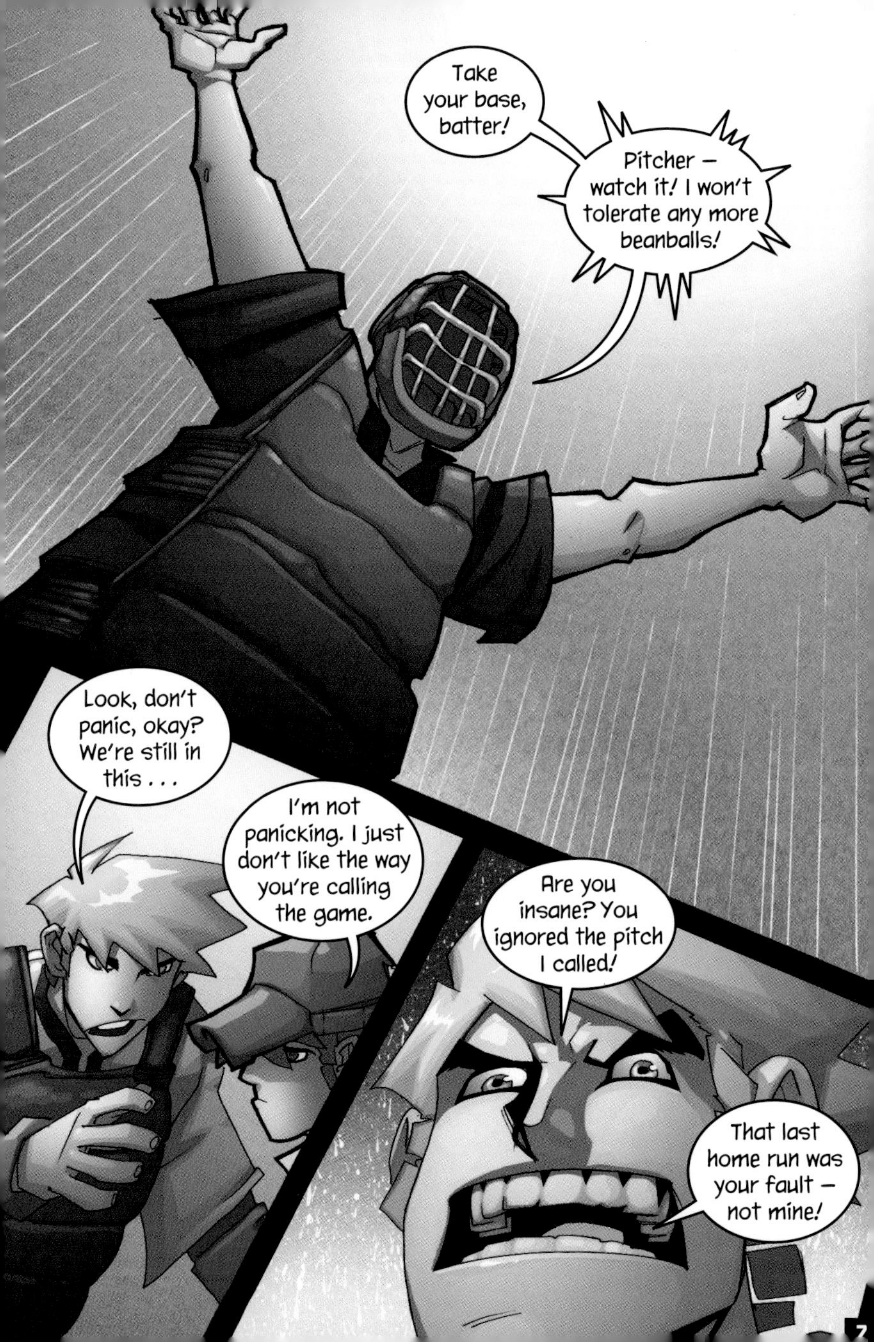
Take your base, batter!
Pitcher — watch it! I won't tolerate any more beanballs!
Look, don't panic, okay? We're still in this . . .
I'm not panicking. I just don't like the way you're calling the game.
Are you insane? You ignored the pitch I called!
That last home run was your fault — not mine!

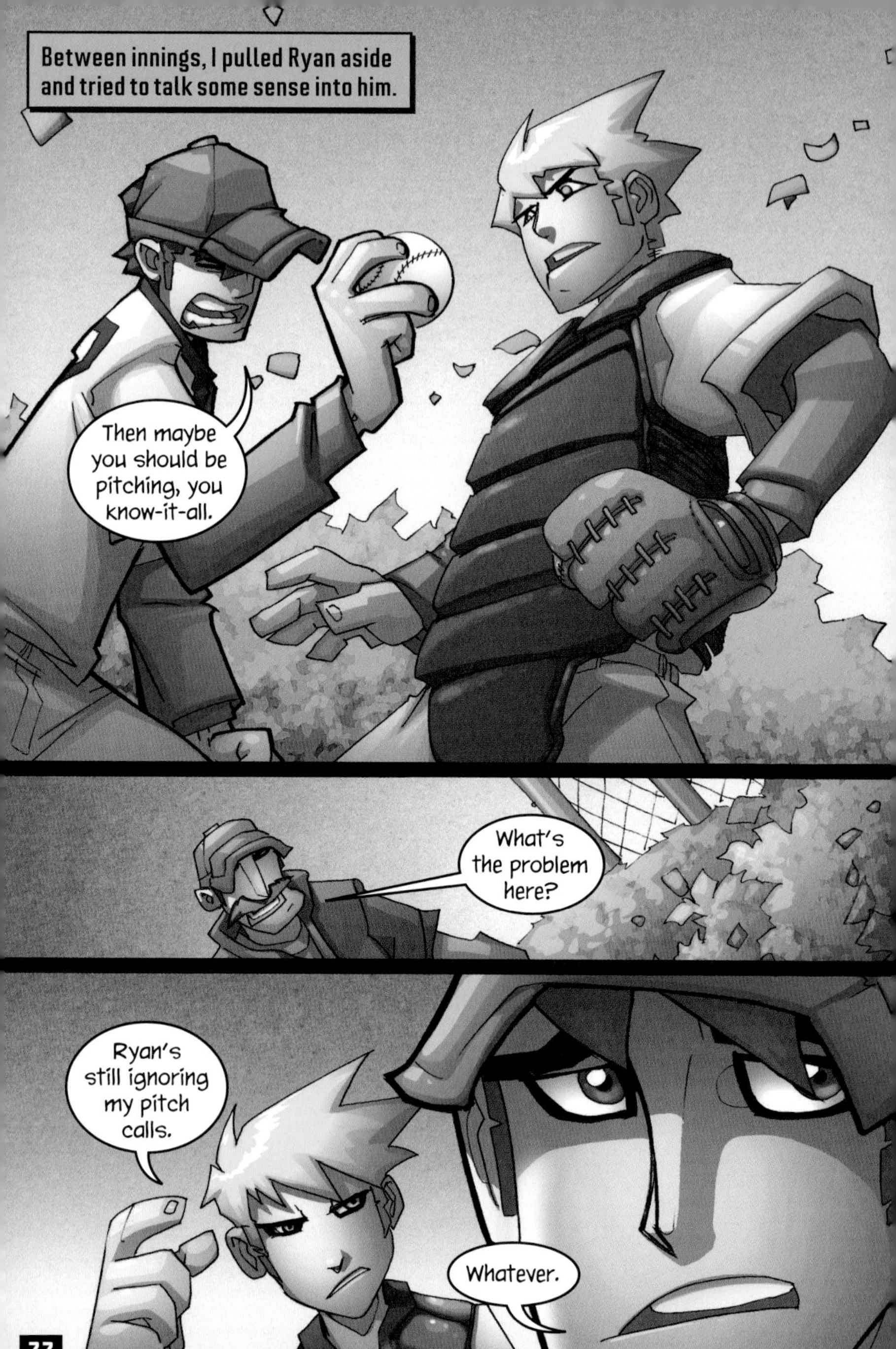

Between innings, I pulled Ryan aside and tried to talk some sense into him.
Then maybe you should be pitching, you know-it-all.
What's the problem here?
Ryan's still ignoring my pitch calls.
Whatever.

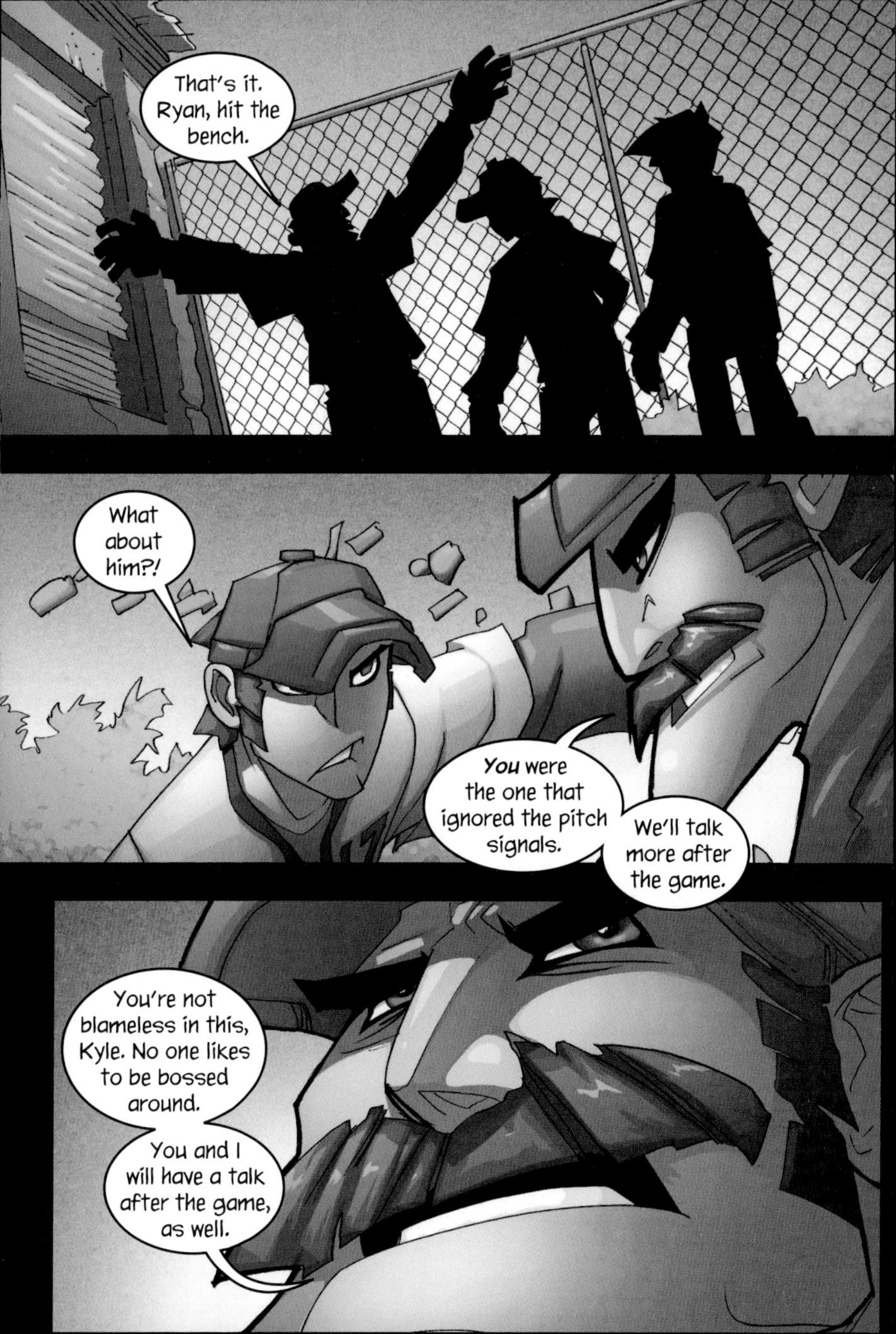
That's it. Ryan, hit the bench.
What about him?!
*You* were the one that ignored the pitch signals.
We'll talk more after the game.
You're not blameless in this, Kyle. No one likes to be bossed around.
You and I will have a talk after the game, as well.

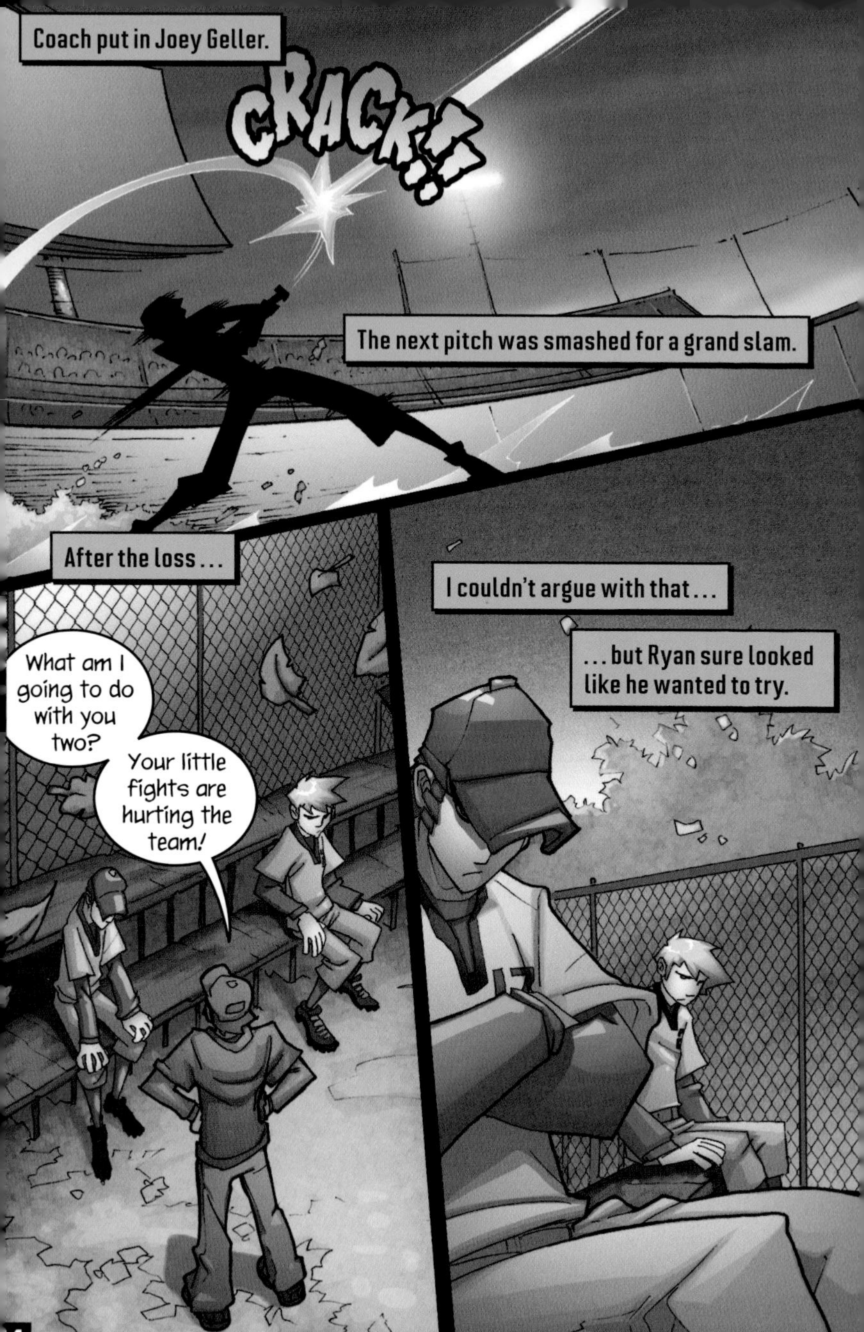
Coach put in Joey Geller.
CRACK!!
The next pitch was smashed for a grand slam.
After the loss . . .
What am I going to do with you two?
Your little fights are hurting the team!
I couldn't argue with that . . .
. . . but Ryan sure looked like he wanted to try.

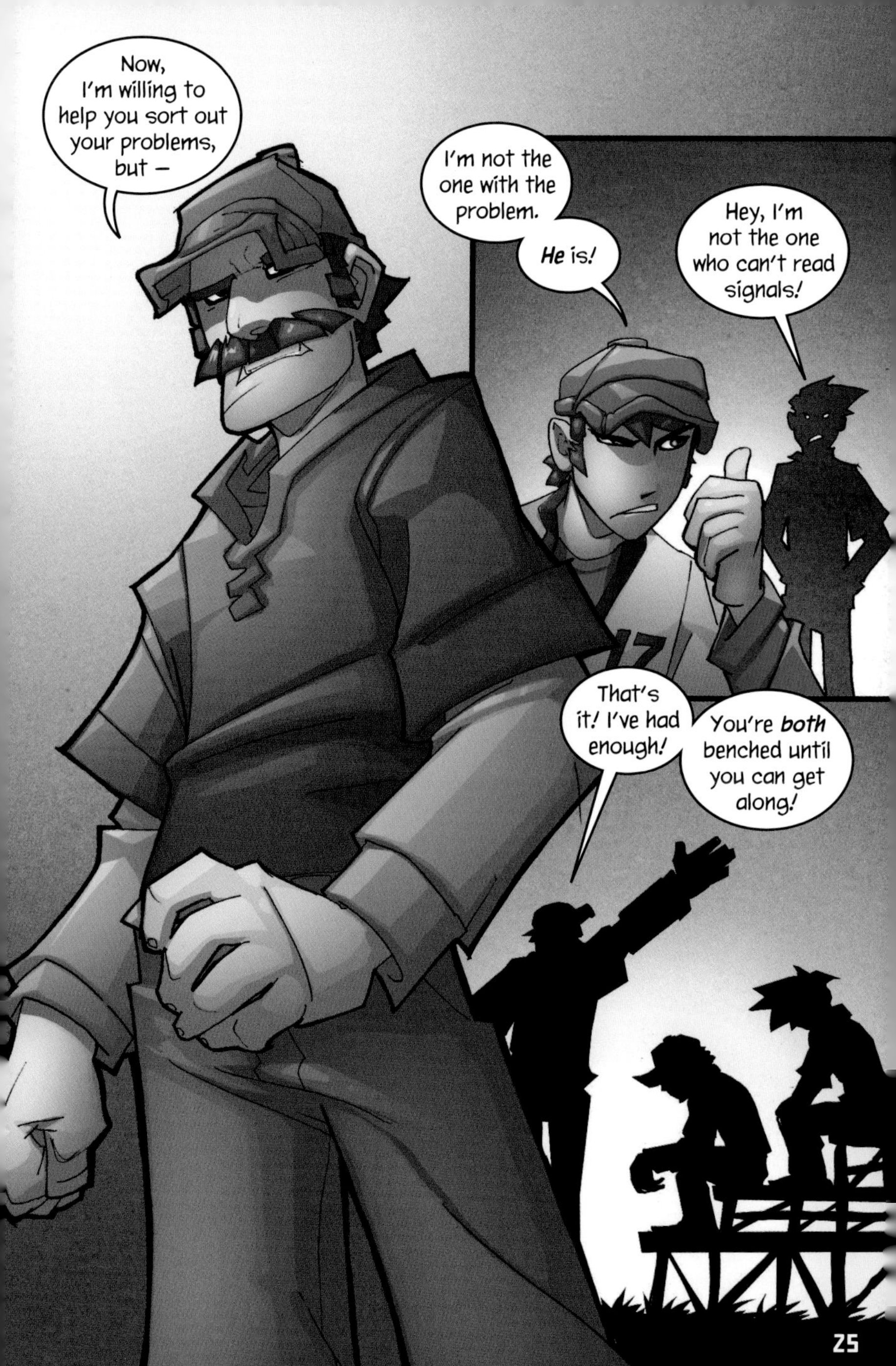
Now, I'm willing to help you sort out your problems, but –
I'm not the one with the problem.
*He* is!
Hey, I'm not the one who can't read signals!
That's it! I've had enough!
You're *both* benched until you can get along!

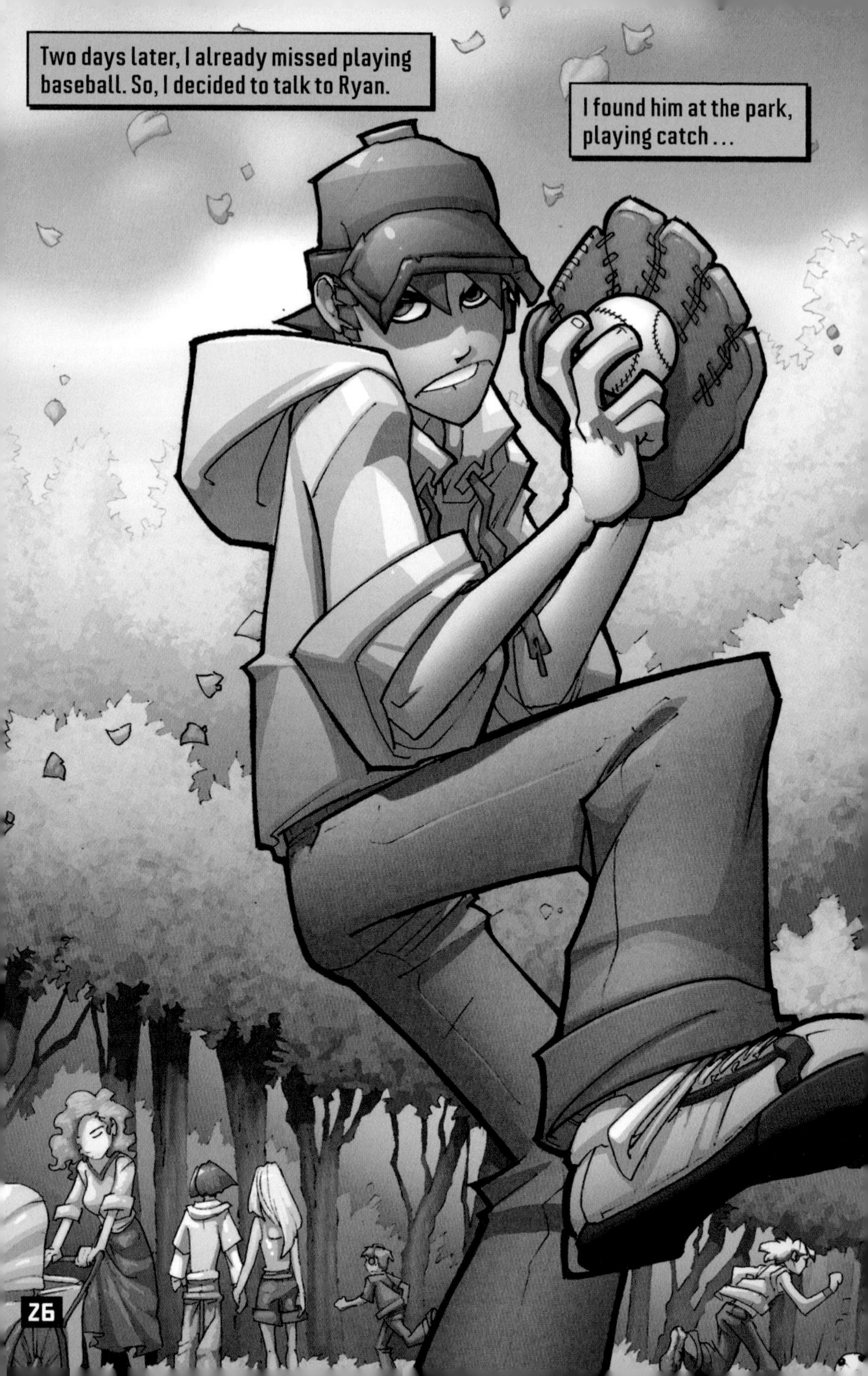
Two days later, I already missed playing baseball. So, I decided to talk to Ryan.
I found him at the park, playing catch . . .

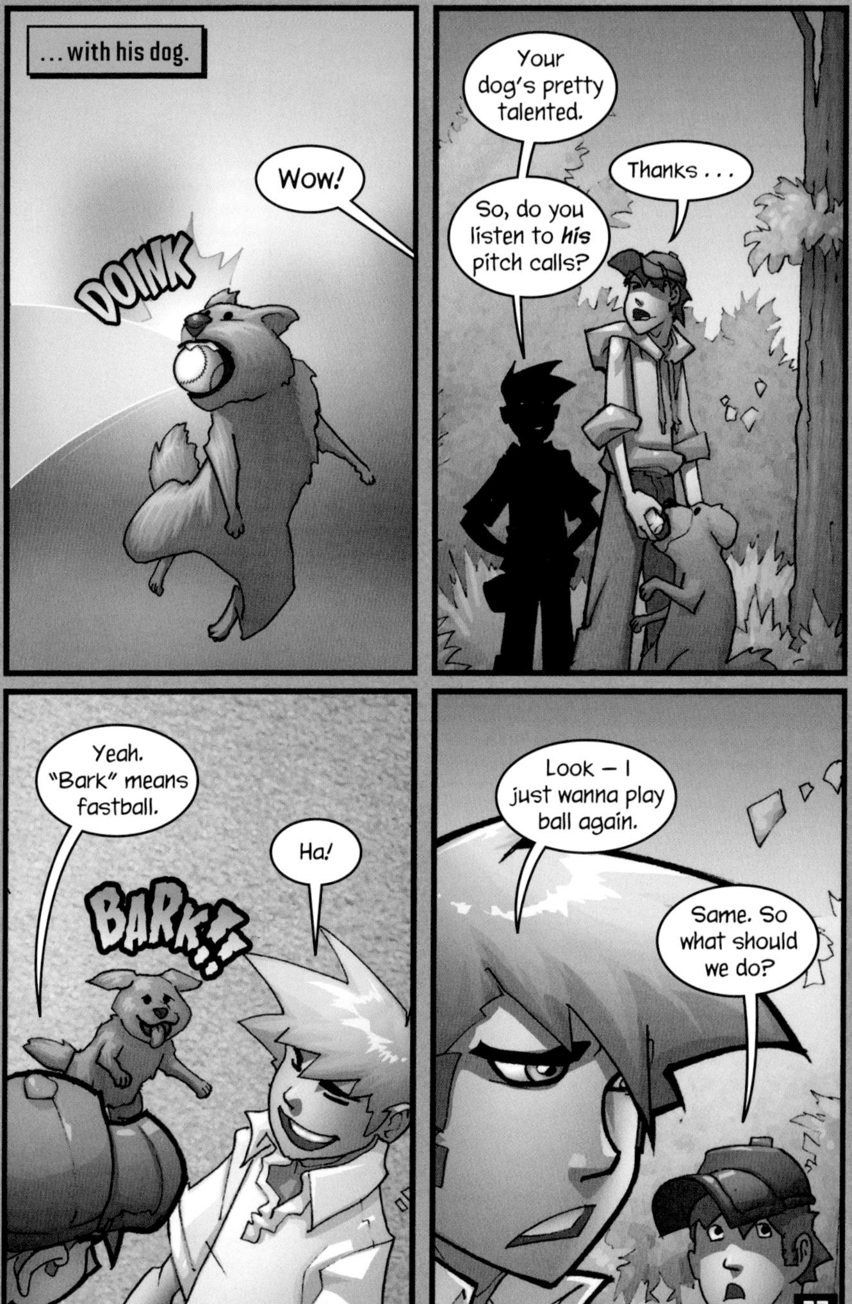
. . . with his dog.
Wow!
DOINK
Your dog's pretty talented.
Thanks . . .
So, do you listen to *his* pitch calls?
Yeah. "Bark" means fastball.
Ha!
BARK!!
Look — I just wanna play ball again.
Same. So what should we do?

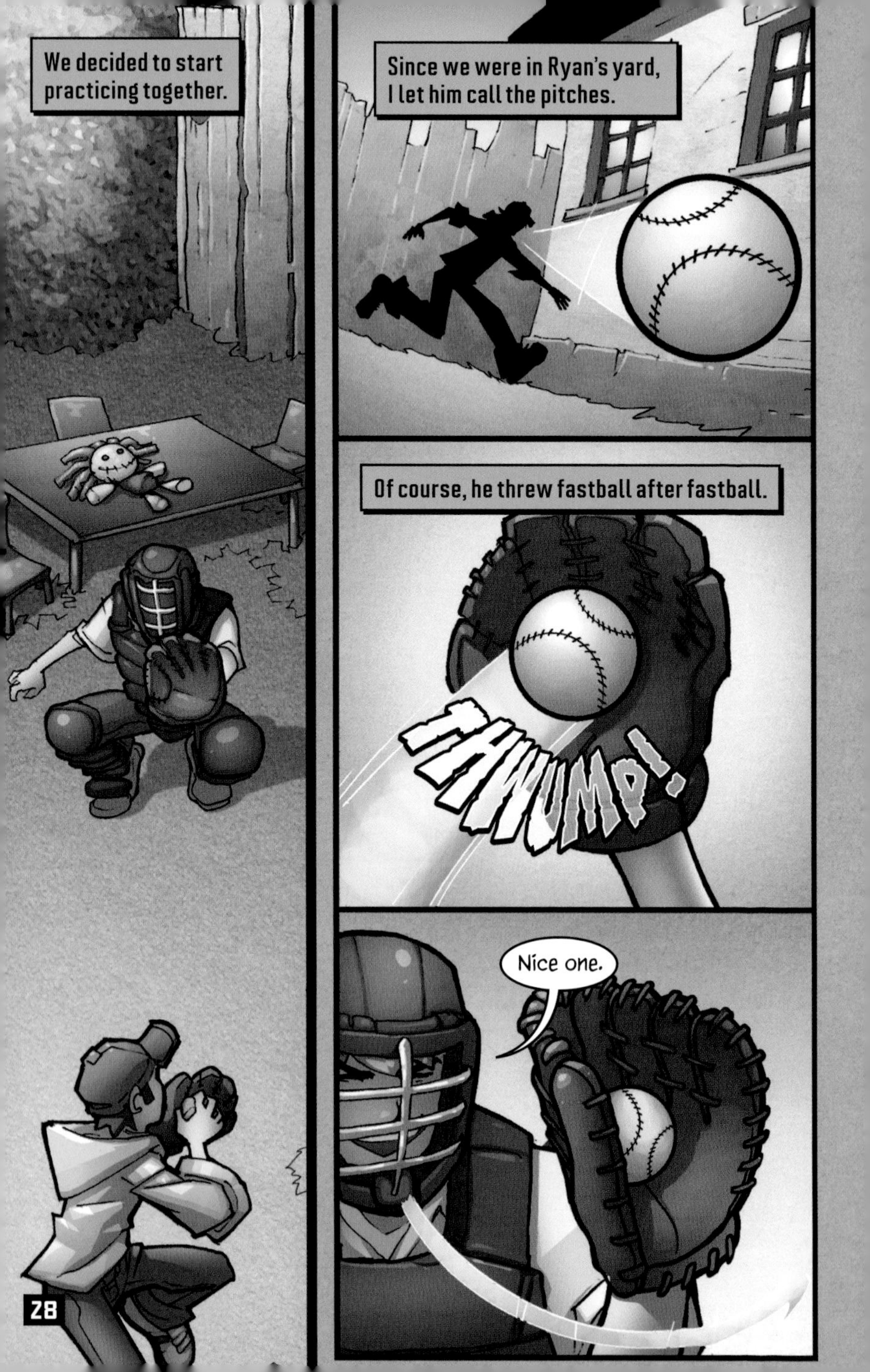

We decided to start practicing together.
Since we were in Ryan's yard, I let him call the pitches.
Of course, he threw fastball after fastball.
THWUMP!
Nice one.

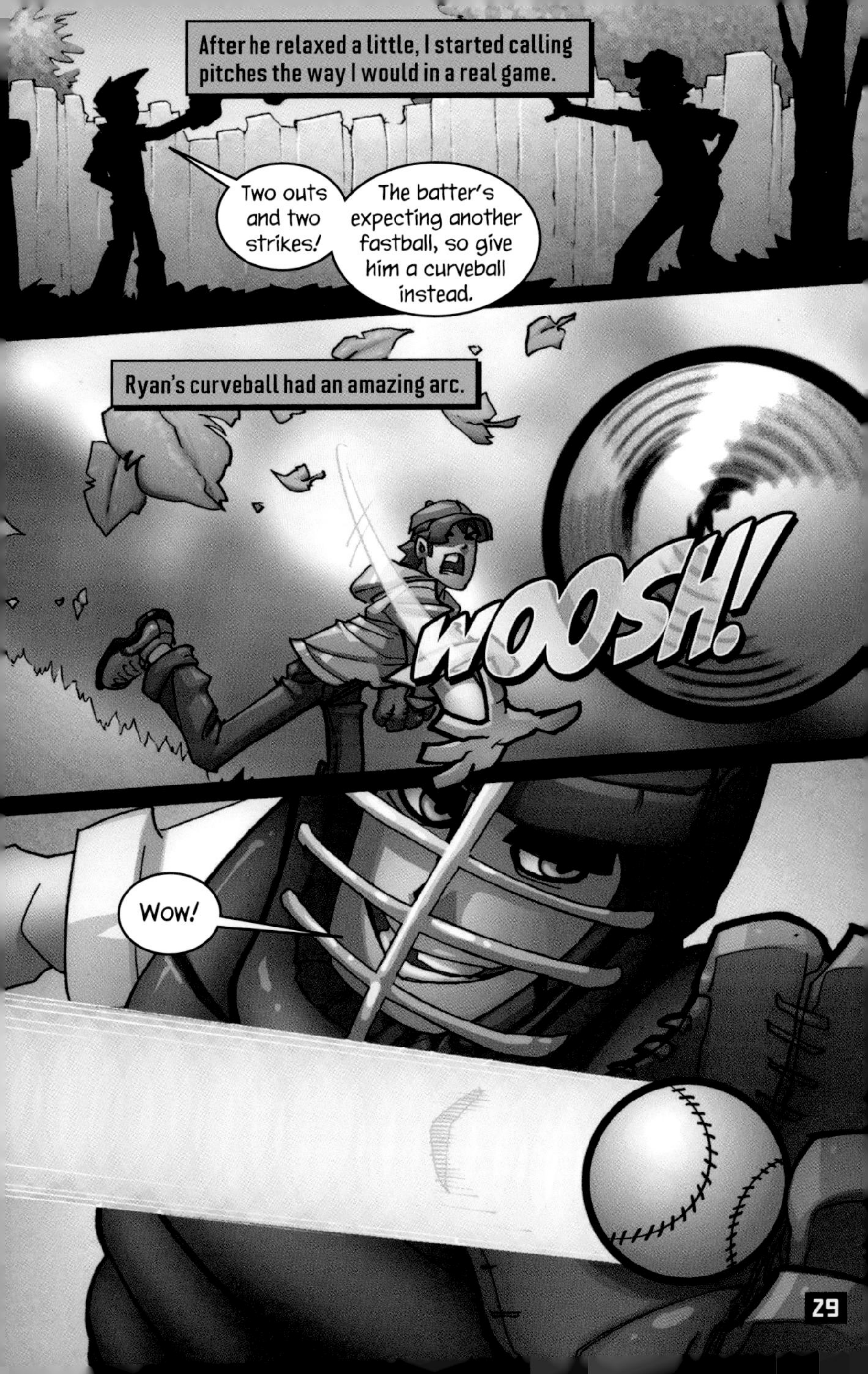
After he relaxed a little, I started calling pitches the way I would in a real game.
Two outs and two strikes!
The batter's expecting another fastball, so give him a curveball instead.
Ryan's curveball had an amazing arc.
WOOSH!
Wow!

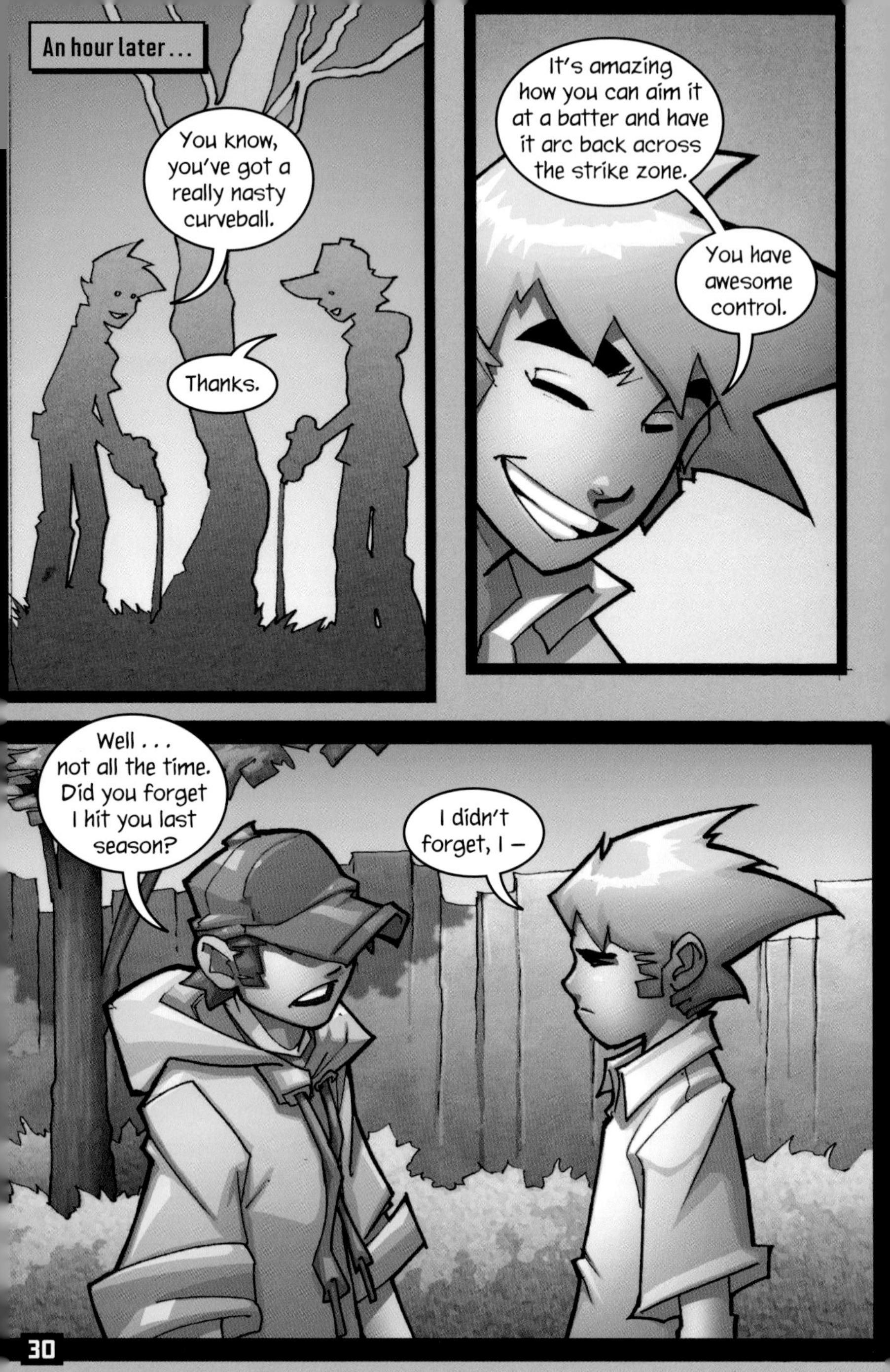
An hour later . . .
You know, you've got a really nasty curveball.
Thanks.
It's amazing how you can aim it at a batter and have it arc back across the strike zone.
You have awesome control.
Well . . . not all the time. Did you forget I hit you last season?
I didn't forget, I –

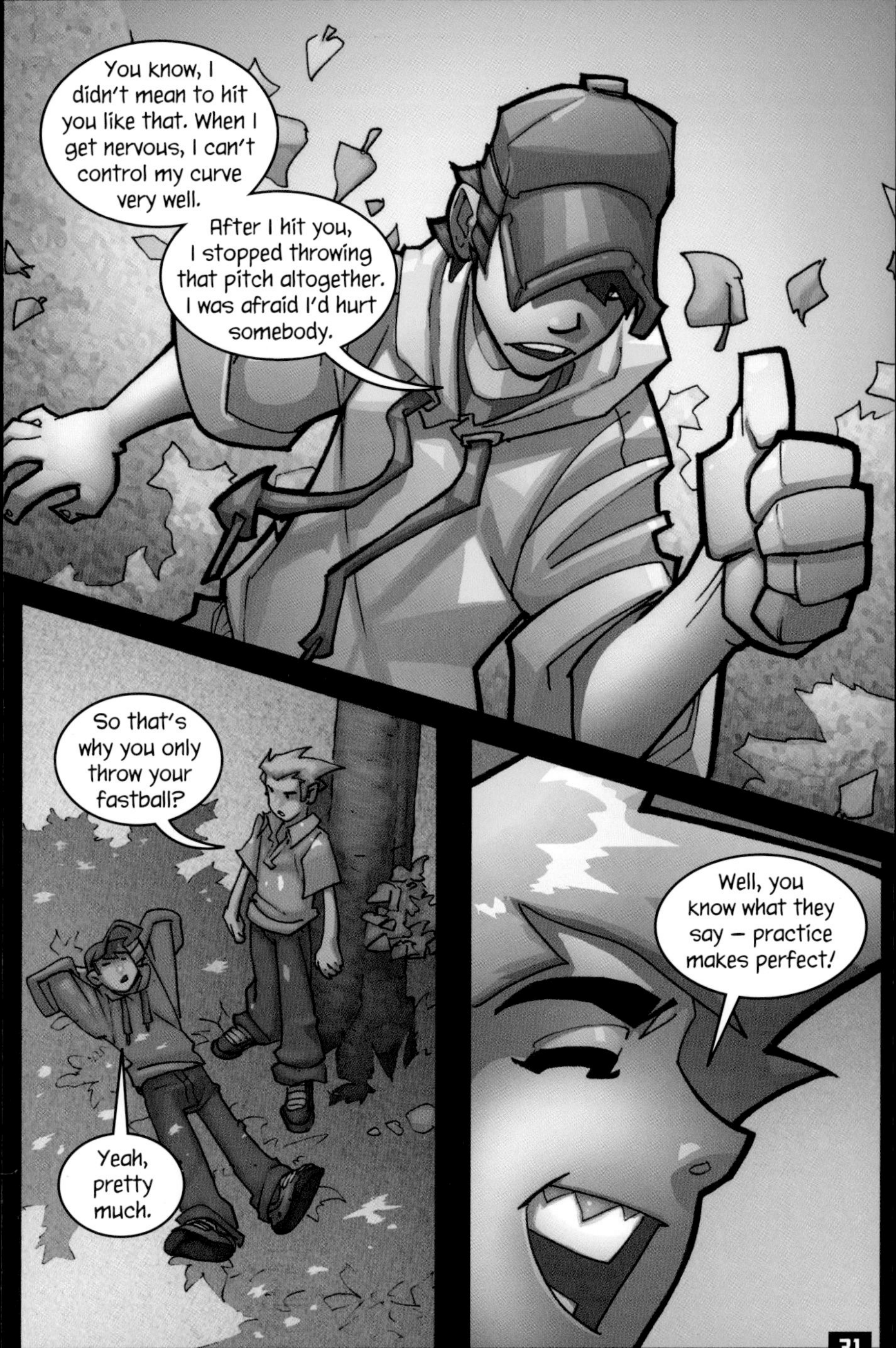
You know, I didn't mean to hit you like that. When I get nervous, I can't control my curve very well.
After I hit you, I stopped throwing that pitch altogether. I was afraid I'd hurt somebody.
So that's why you only throw your fastball?
Yeah, pretty much.
Well, you know what they say — practice makes perfect!

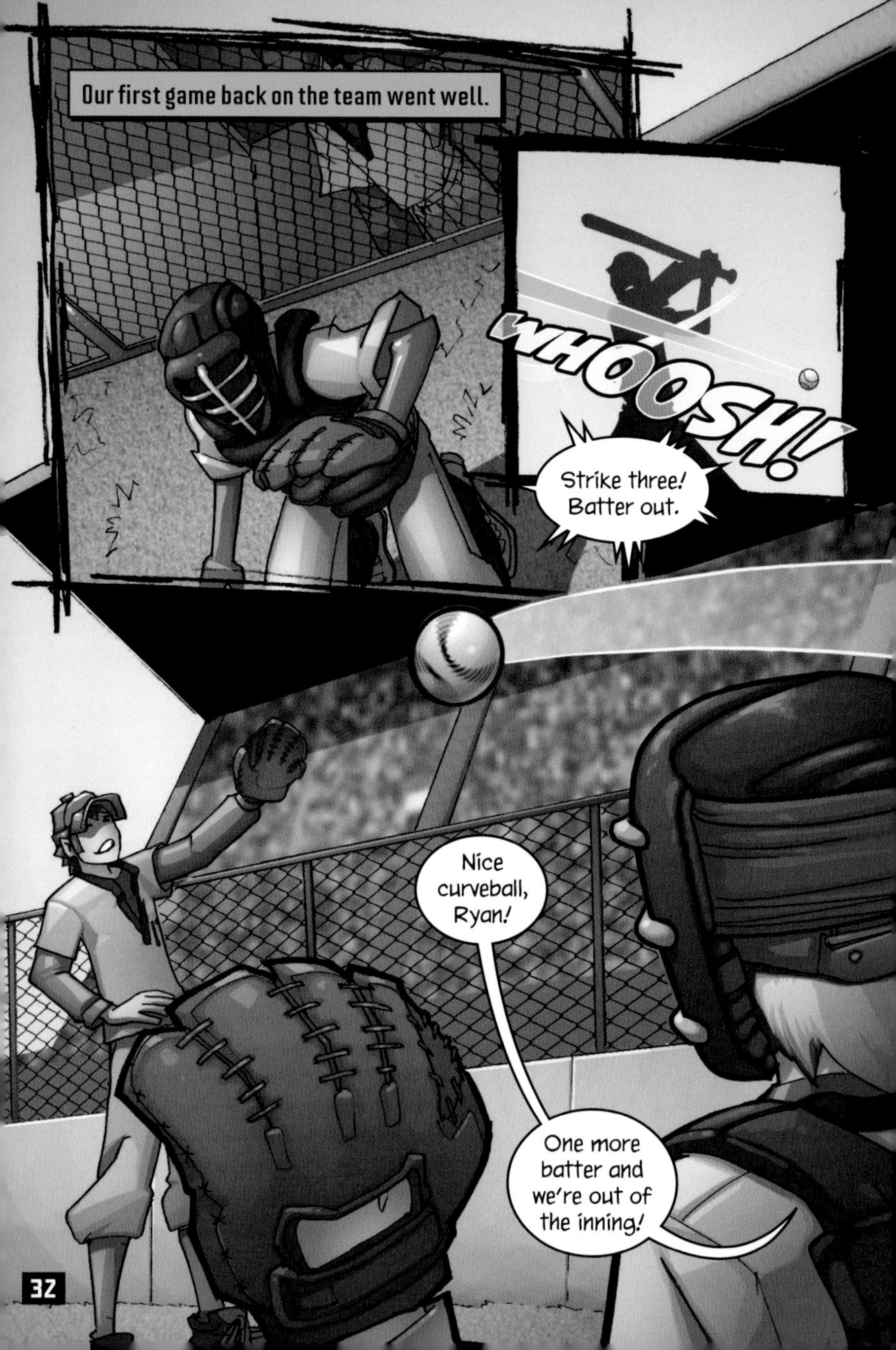
Our first game back on the team went well.
WHOOSH!
Strike three! Batter out.
Nice curveball, Ryan!
One more batter and we're out of the inning!

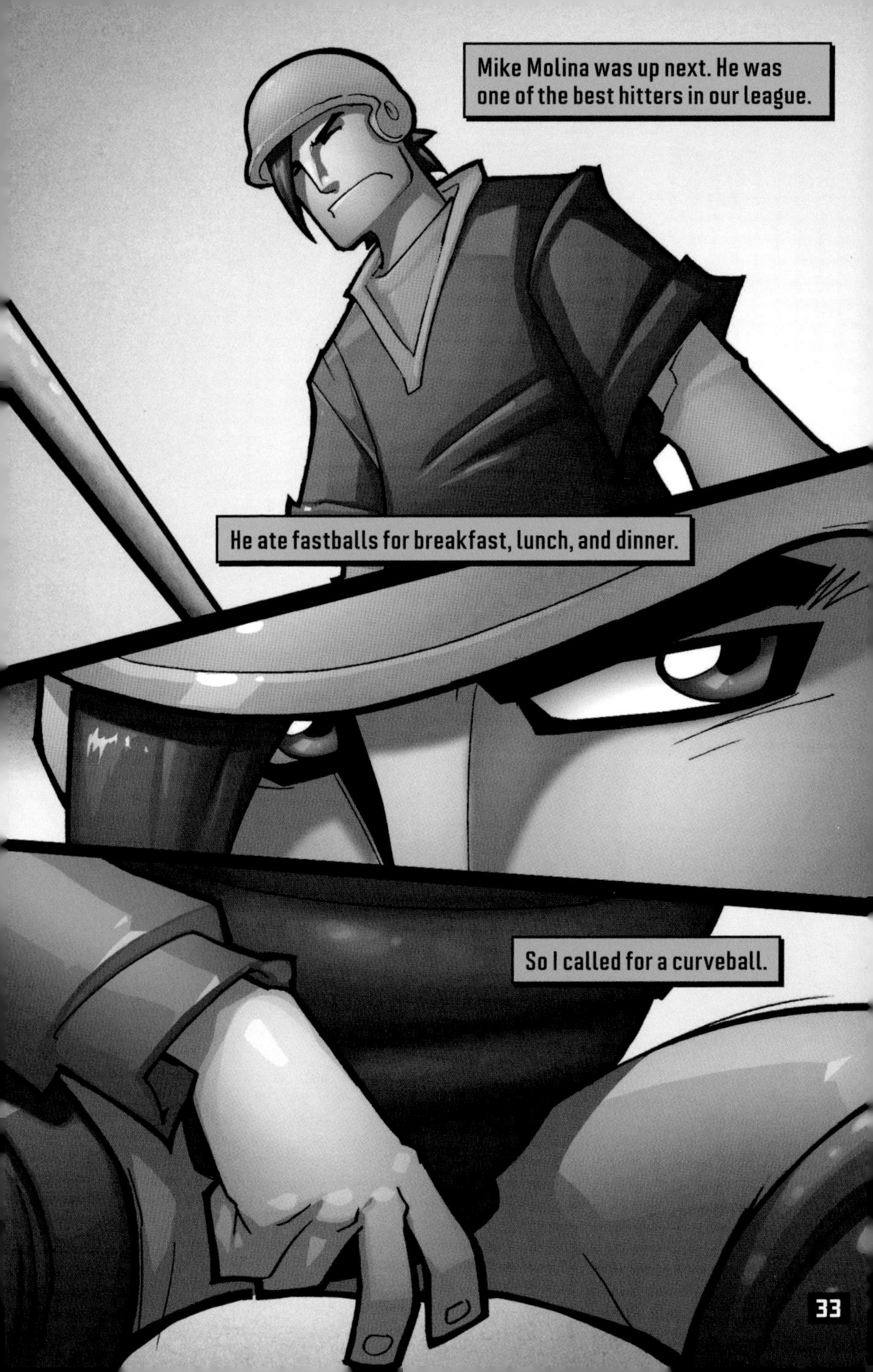
Mike Molina was up next. He was one of the best hitters in our league.
He ate fastballs for breakfast, lunch, and dinner.
So I called for a curveball.

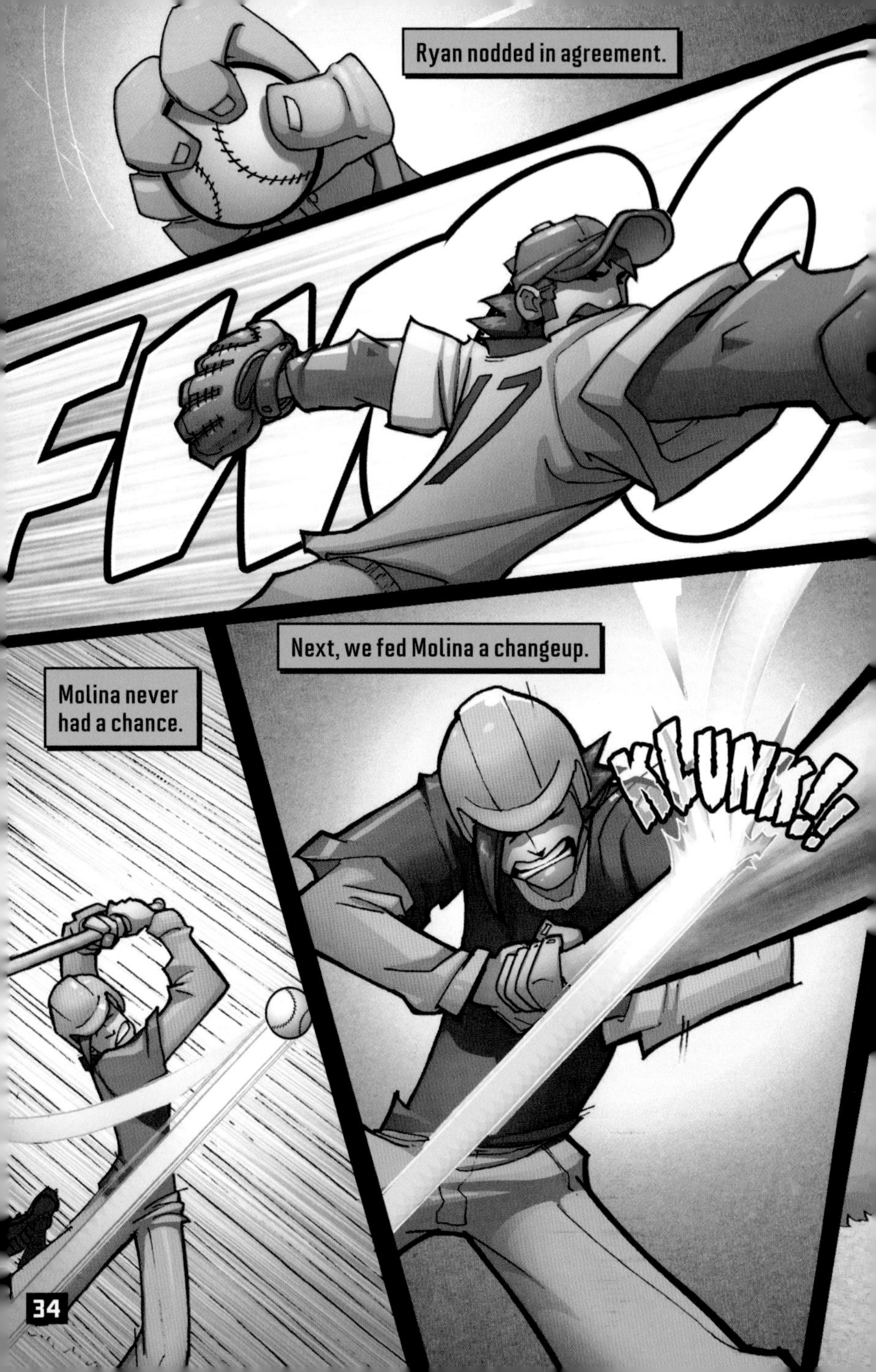
Ryan nodded in agreement.
Next, we fed Molina a changeup.
Molina never had a chance.
KLUNK!!

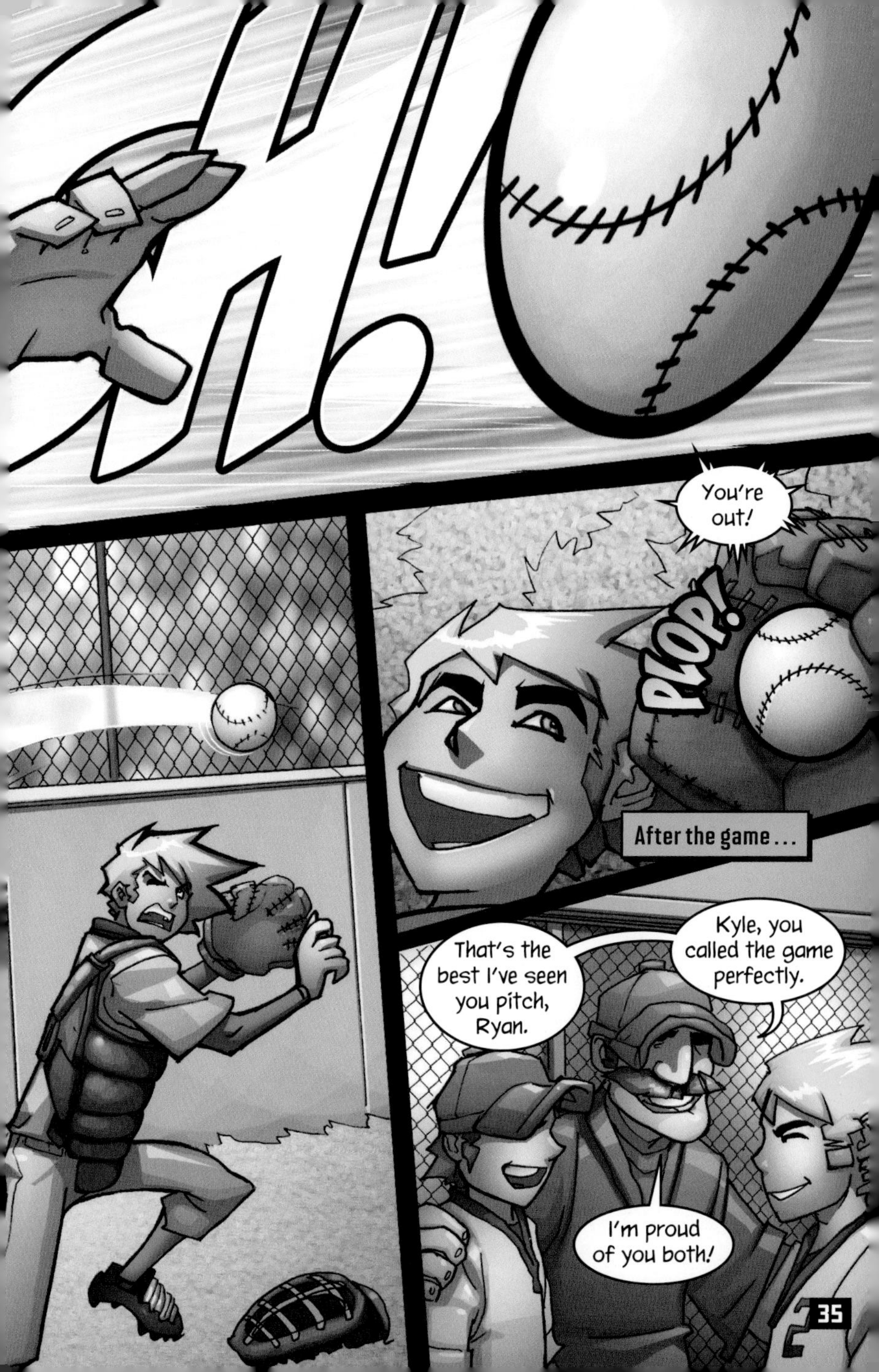

You're out!
PLOP!
After the game . . .
That's the best I've seen you pitch, Ryan.
Kyle, you called the game perfectly.
I'm proud of you both!

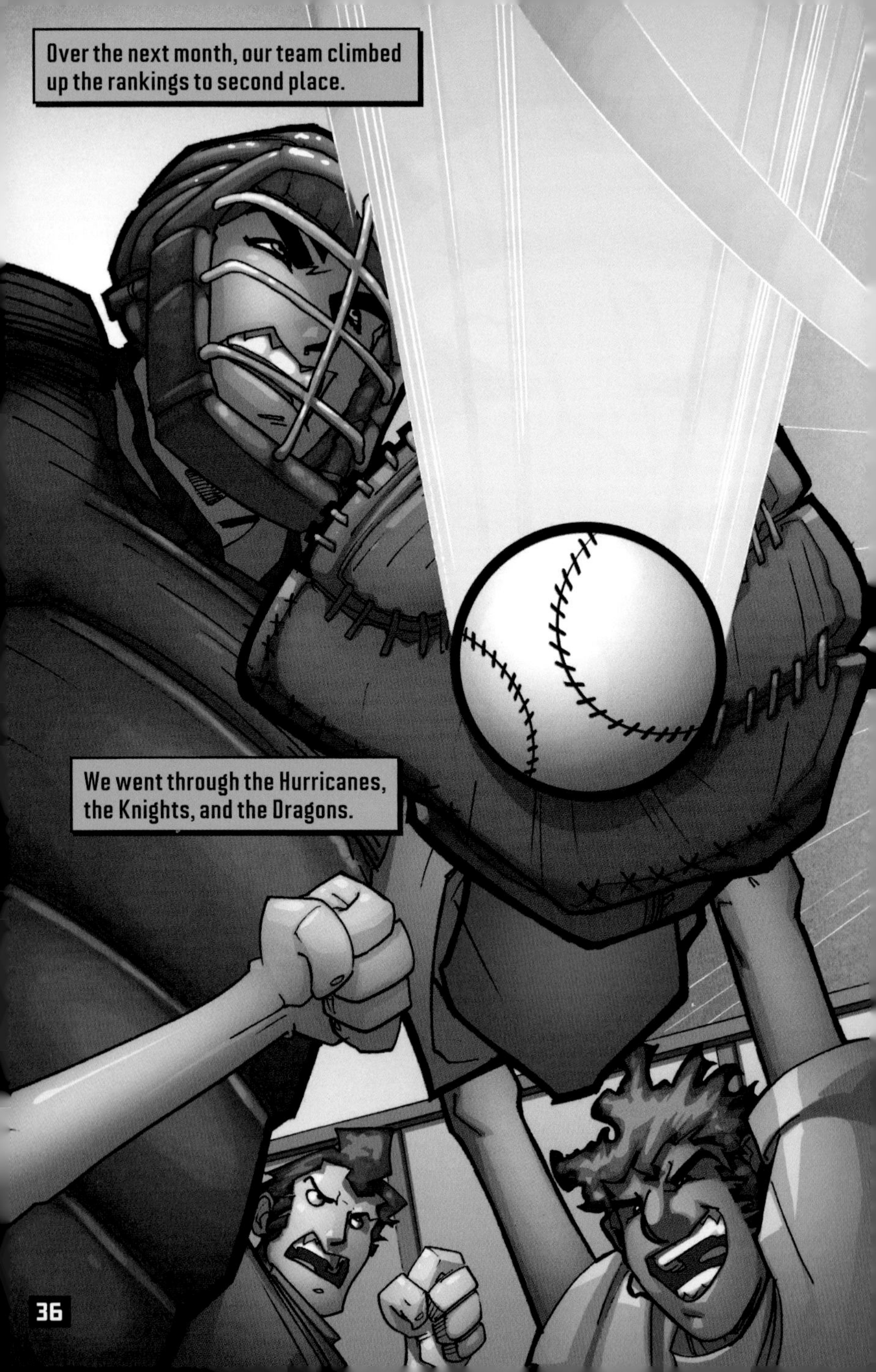
Over the next month, our team climbed up the rankings to second place.
We went through the Hurricanes, the Knights, and the Dragons.

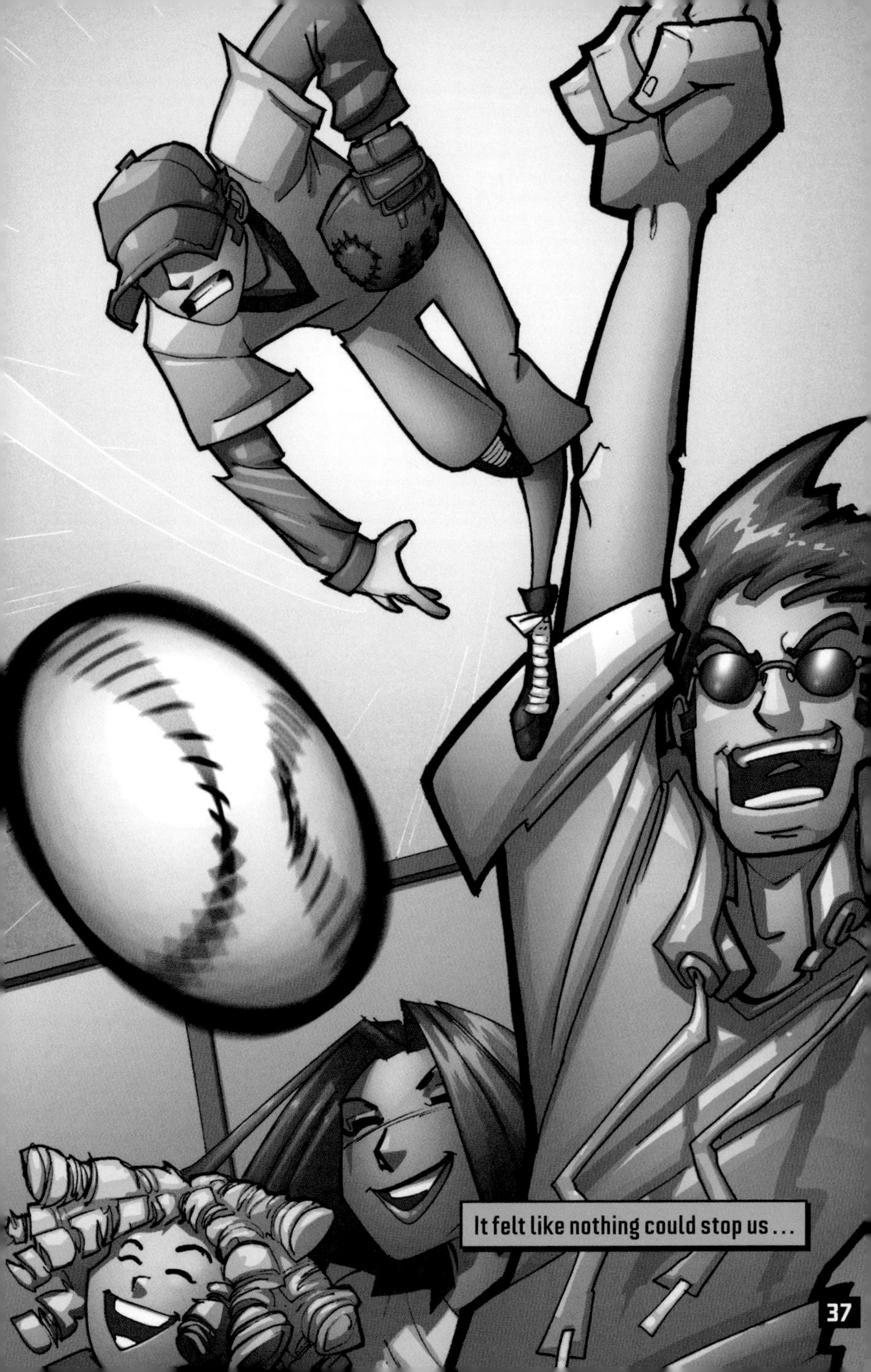
It felt like nothing could stop us . . .

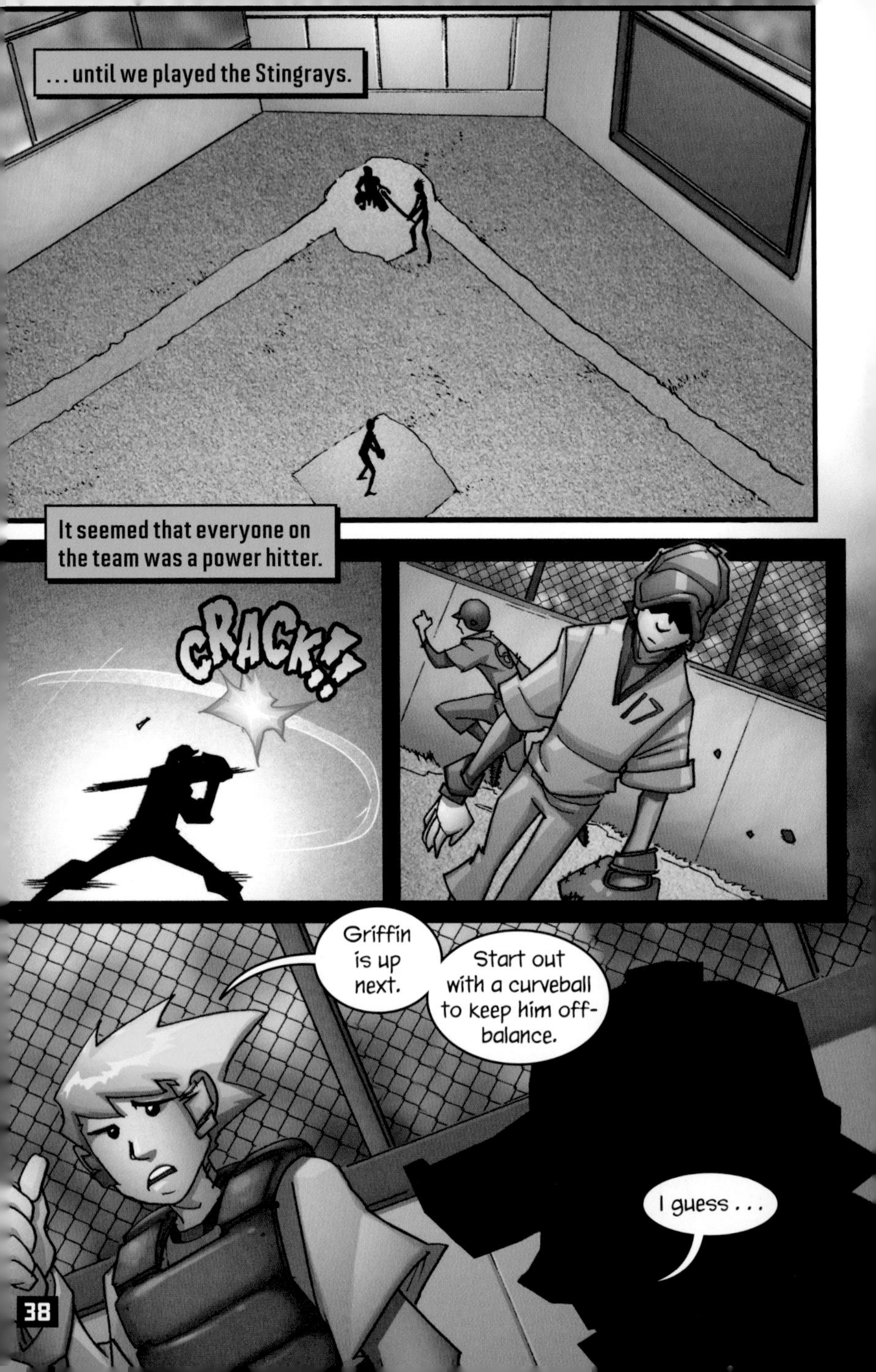
... until we played the Stingrays.
It seemed that everyone on the team was a power hitter.
CRACK!!
Griffin is up next.
Start out with a curveball to keep him off-balance.
I guess . . .

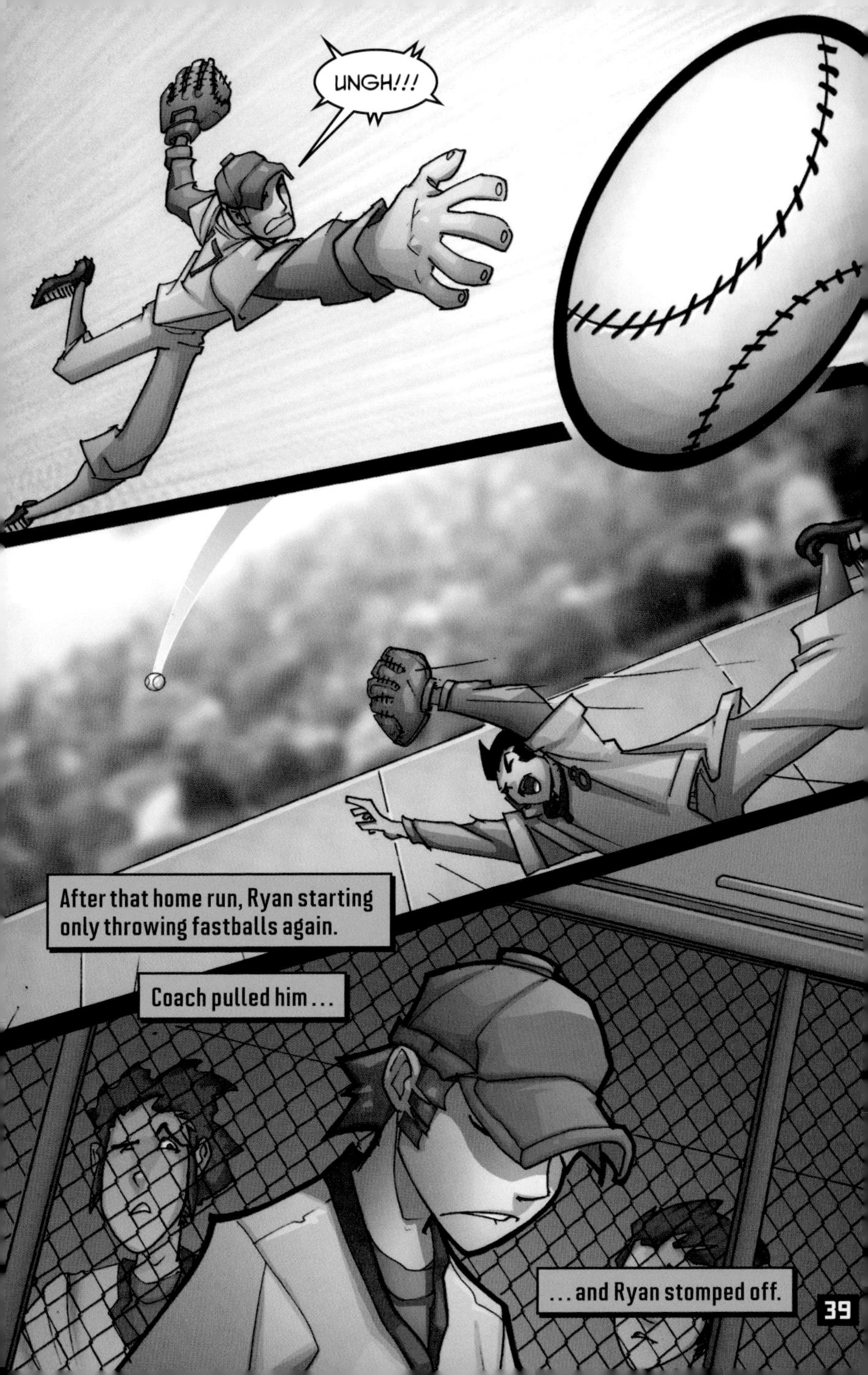

UNGH!!!
After that home run, Ryan starting only throwing fastballs again.
Coach pulled him . . .
. . . and Ryan stomped off.

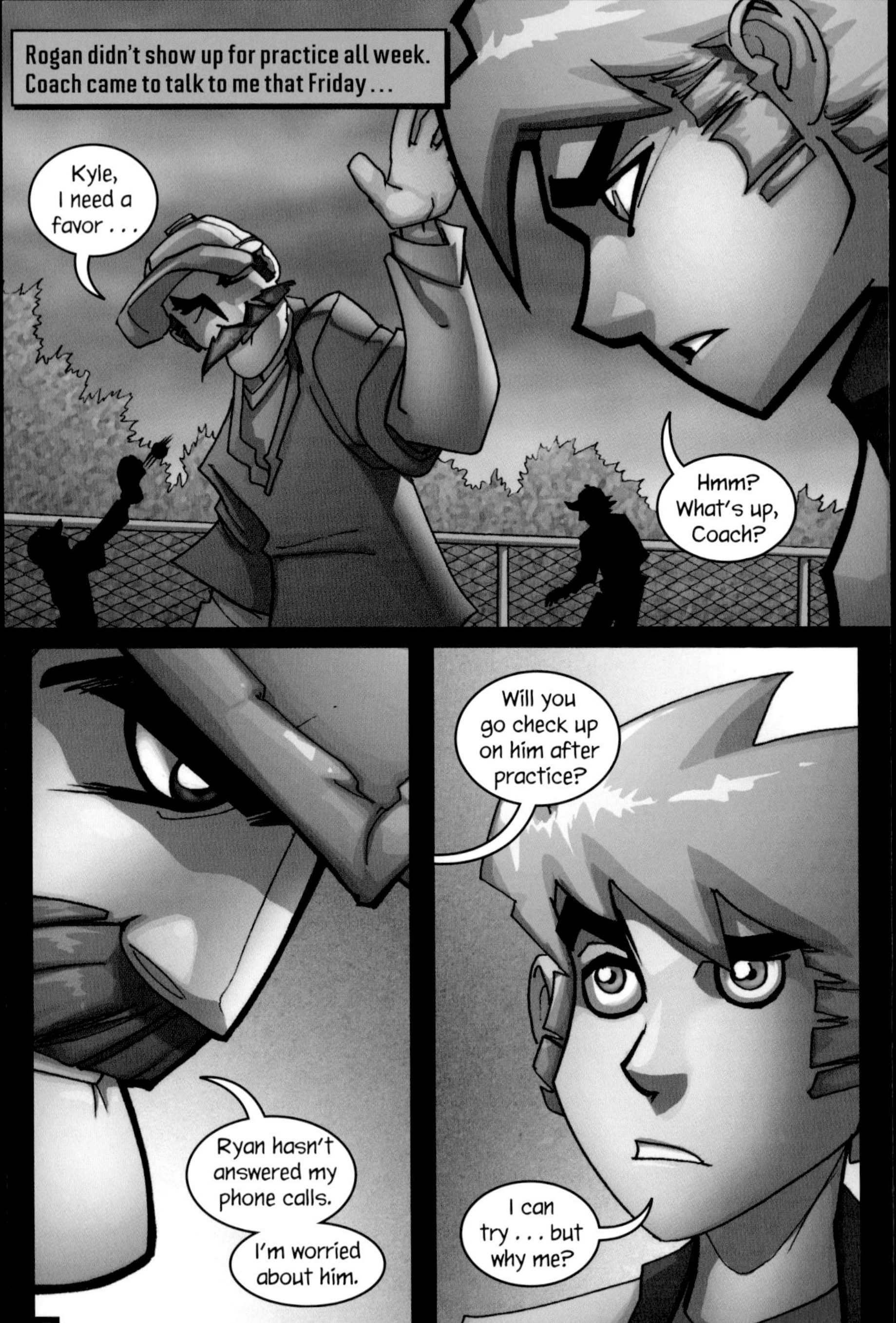
Rogan didn't show up for practice all week. Coach came to talk to me that Friday . . .
Kyle, I need a favor . . .
Hmm? What's up, Coach?
Will you go check up on him after practice?
Ryan hasn't answered my phone calls.
I'm worried about him.
I can try . . . but why me?

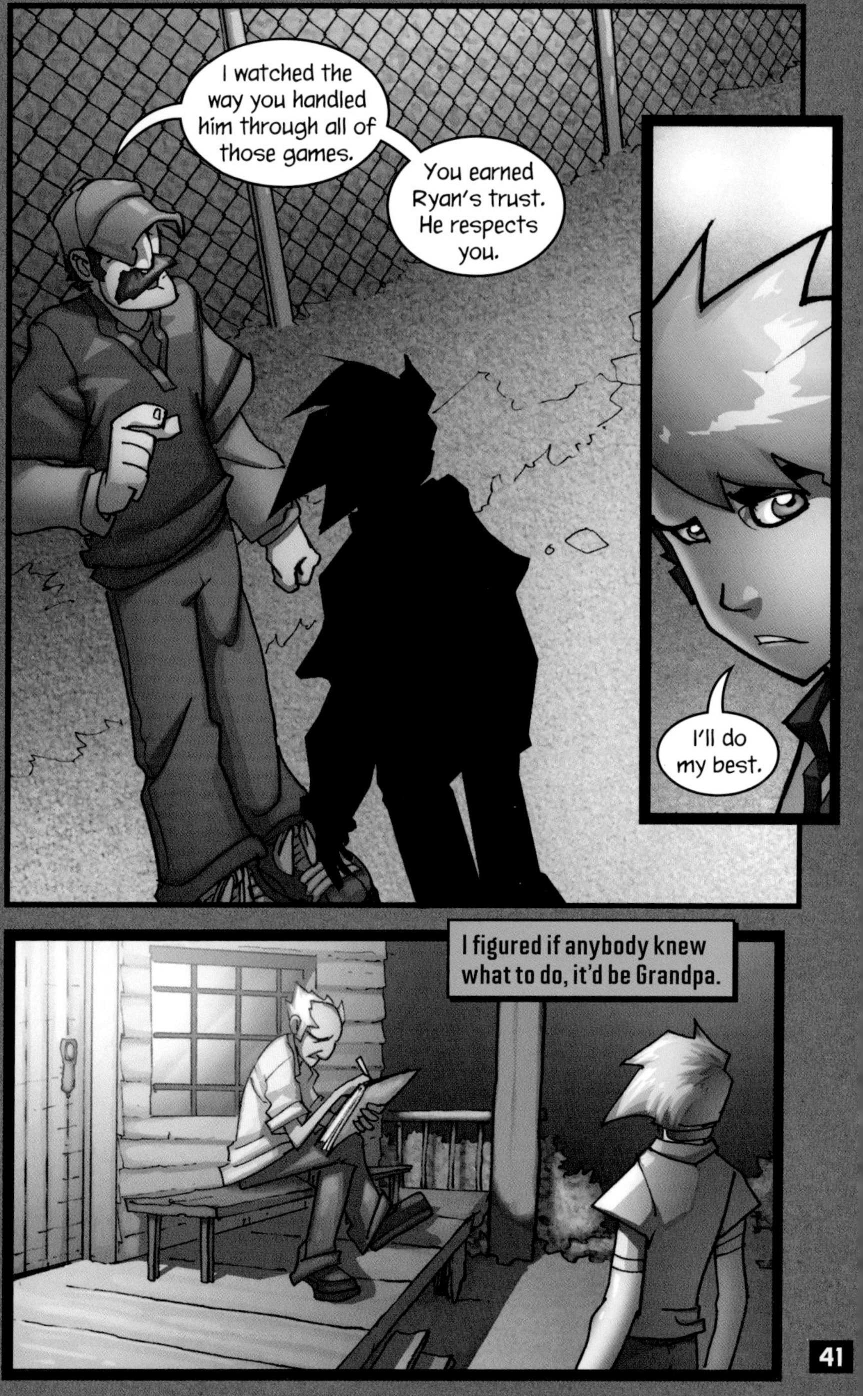
I watched the way you handled him through all of those games.
You earned Ryan's trust. He respects you.
I'll do my best.
I figured if anybody knew what to do, it'd be Grandpa.

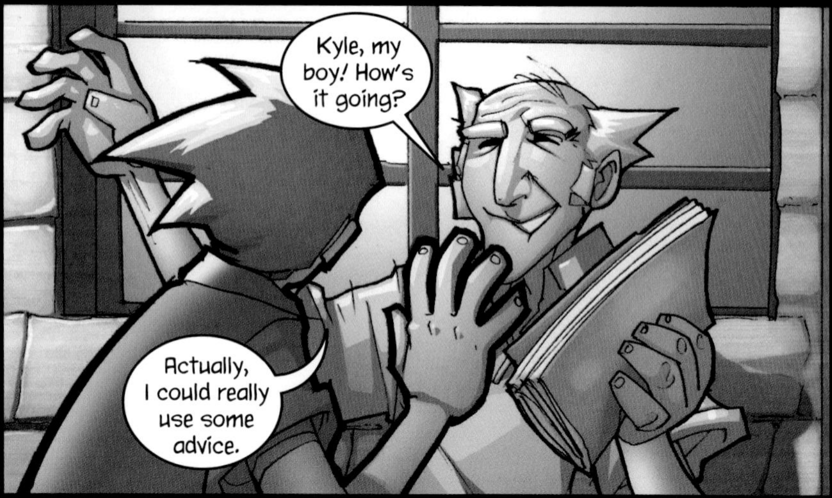
Kyle, my boy! How's it going?
Actually, I could really use some advice.

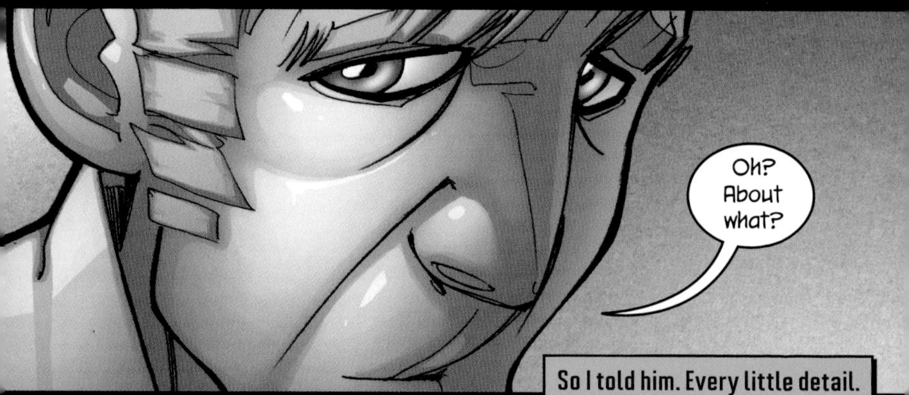
Oh? About what?
So I told him. Every little detail.

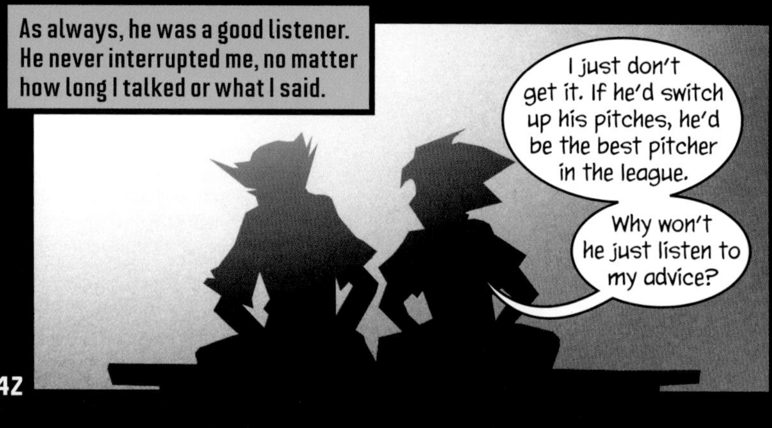
As always, he was a good listener. He never interrupted me, no matter how long I talked or what I said.
I just don't get it. If he'd switch up his pitches, he'd be the best pitcher in the league.
Why won't he just listen to my advice?

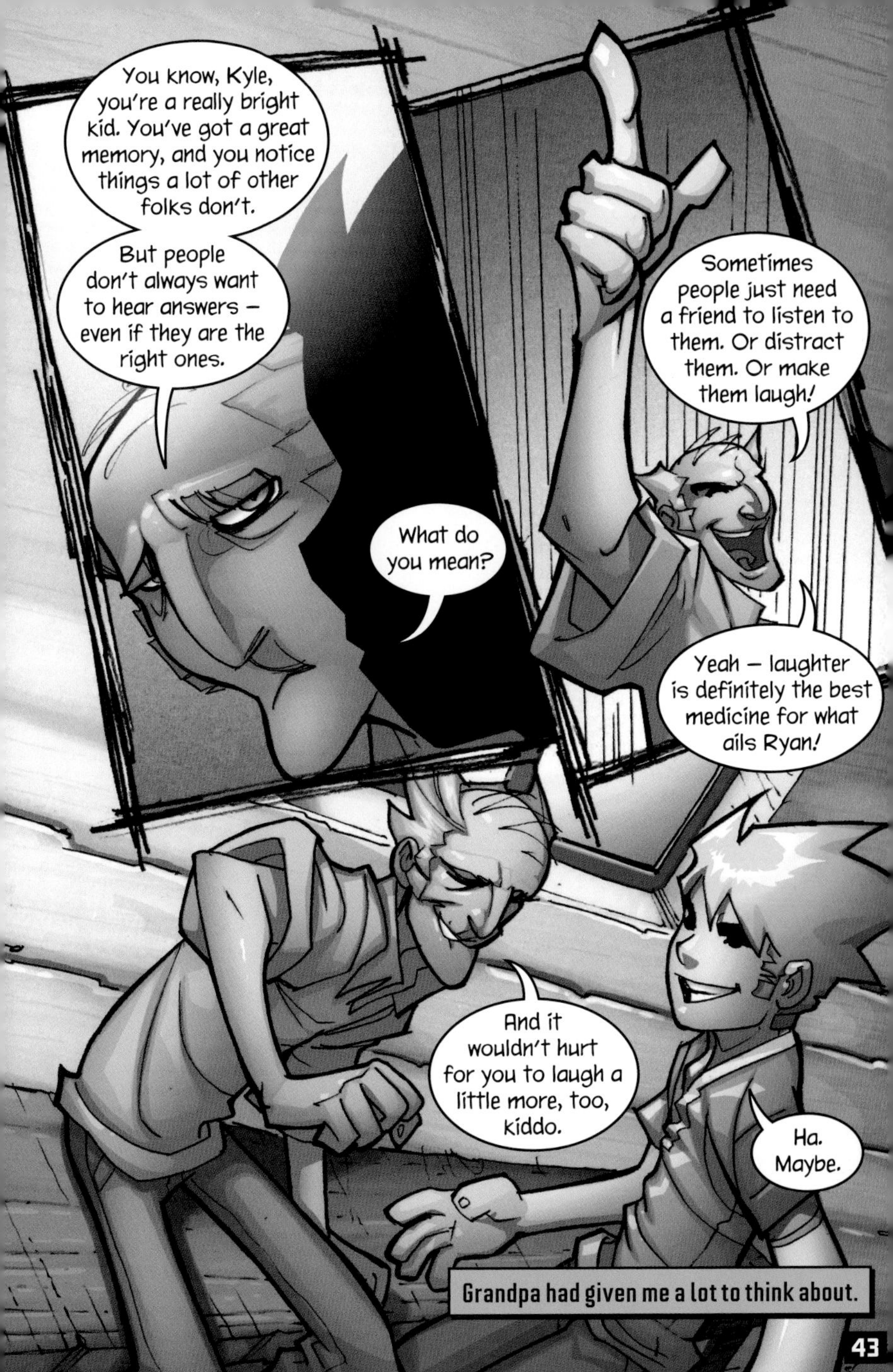

You know, Kyle, you're a really bright kid. You've got a great memory, and you notice things a lot of other folks don't.
But people don't always want to hear answers — even if they are the right ones.
Sometimes people just need a friend to listen to them. Or distract them. Or make them laugh!
What do you mean?
Yeah — laughter is definitely the best medicine for what ails Ryan!
And it wouldn't hurt for you to laugh a little more, too, kiddo.
Ha. Maybe.
Grandpa had given me a lot to think about.

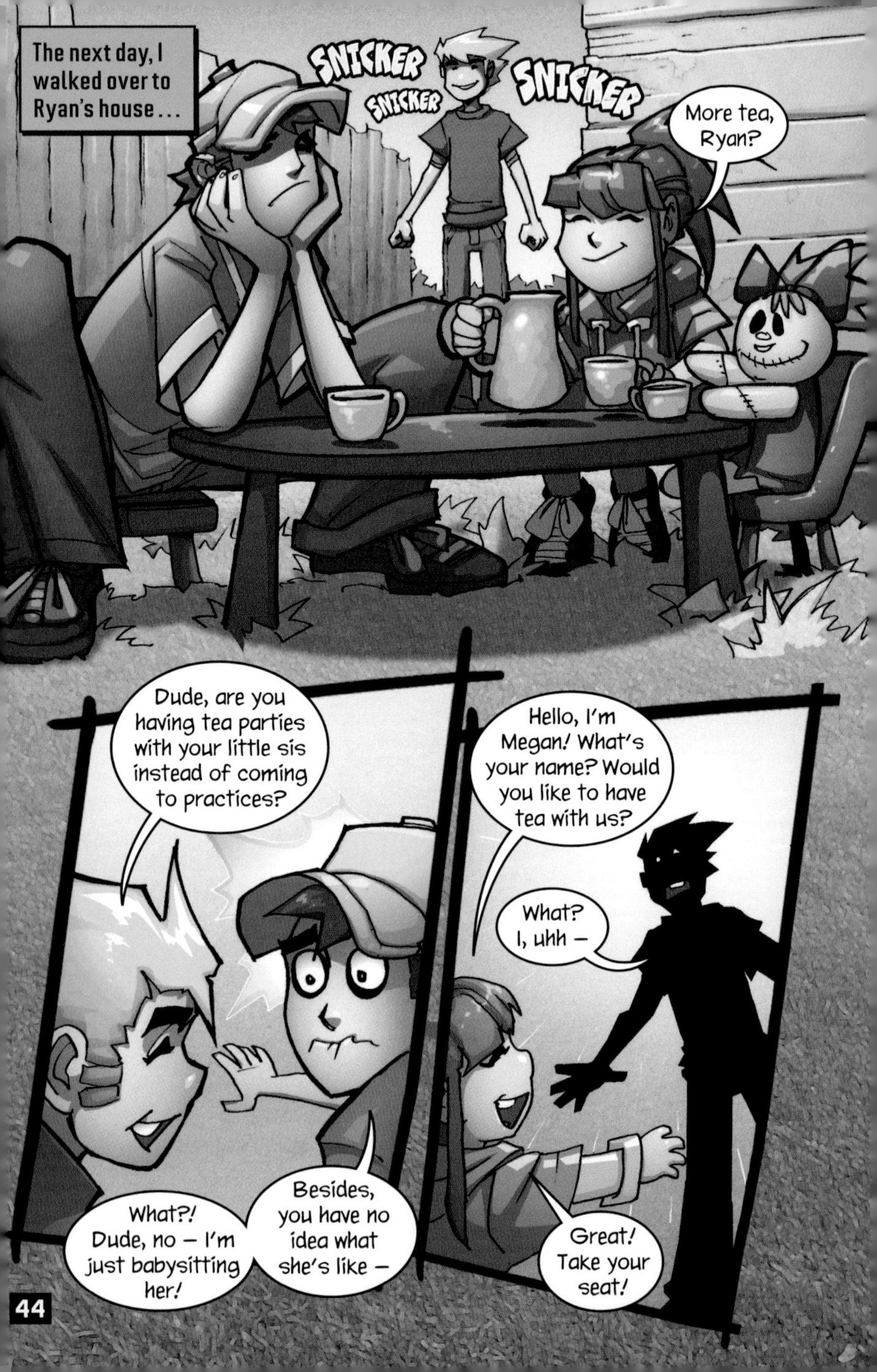

The next day, I walked over to Ryan's house . . .
SNICKER
SNICKER
SNICKER
More tea, Ryan?
Dude, are you having tea parties with your little sis instead of coming to practices?
What?! Dude, no — I'm just babysitting her!
Besides, you have no idea what she's like —
Hello, I'm Megan! What's your name? Would you like to have tea with us?
What? I, uhh —
Great! Take your seat!

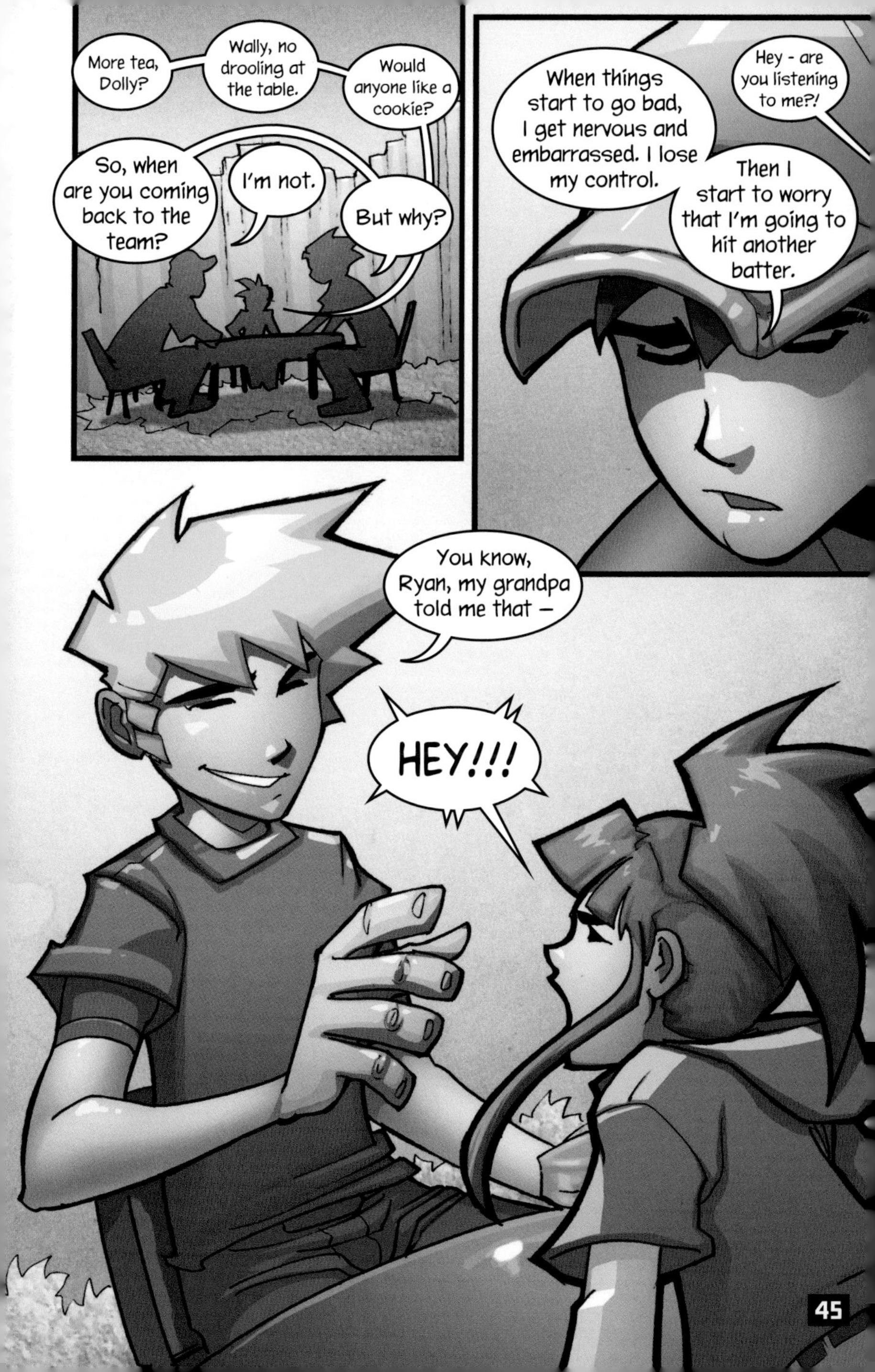
More tea, Dolly?
Wally, no drooling at the table.
Would anyone like a cookie?
So, when are you coming back to the team?
I'm not.
But why?
When things start to go bad, I get nervous and embarrassed. I lose my control.
Hey - are you listening to me?!
Then I start to worry that I'm going to hit another batter.
You know, Ryan, my grandpa told me that –
HEY!!!
45

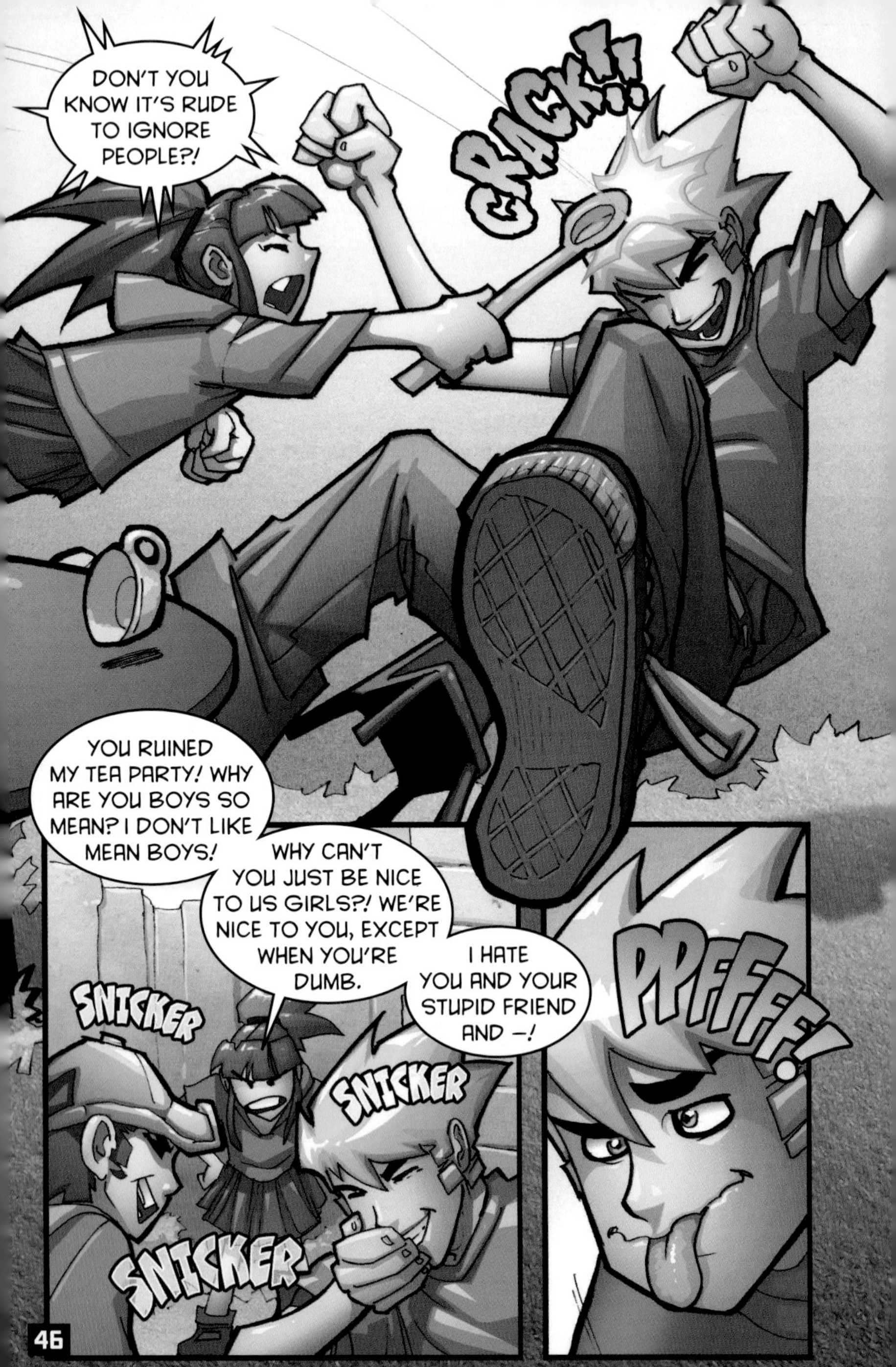
DON'T YOU KNOW IT'S RUDE TO IGNORE PEOPLE?!
CRACK!!!
YOU RUINED MY TEA PARTY! WHY ARE YOU BOYS SO MEAN? I DON'T LIKE MEAN BOYS!
WHY CAN'T YOU JUST BE NICE TO US GIRLS?! WE'RE NICE TO YOU, EXCEPT WHEN YOU'RE DUMB.
I HATE YOU AND YOUR STUPID FRIEND AND –!
SNICKER
SNICKER
SNICKER
PPFFFF!

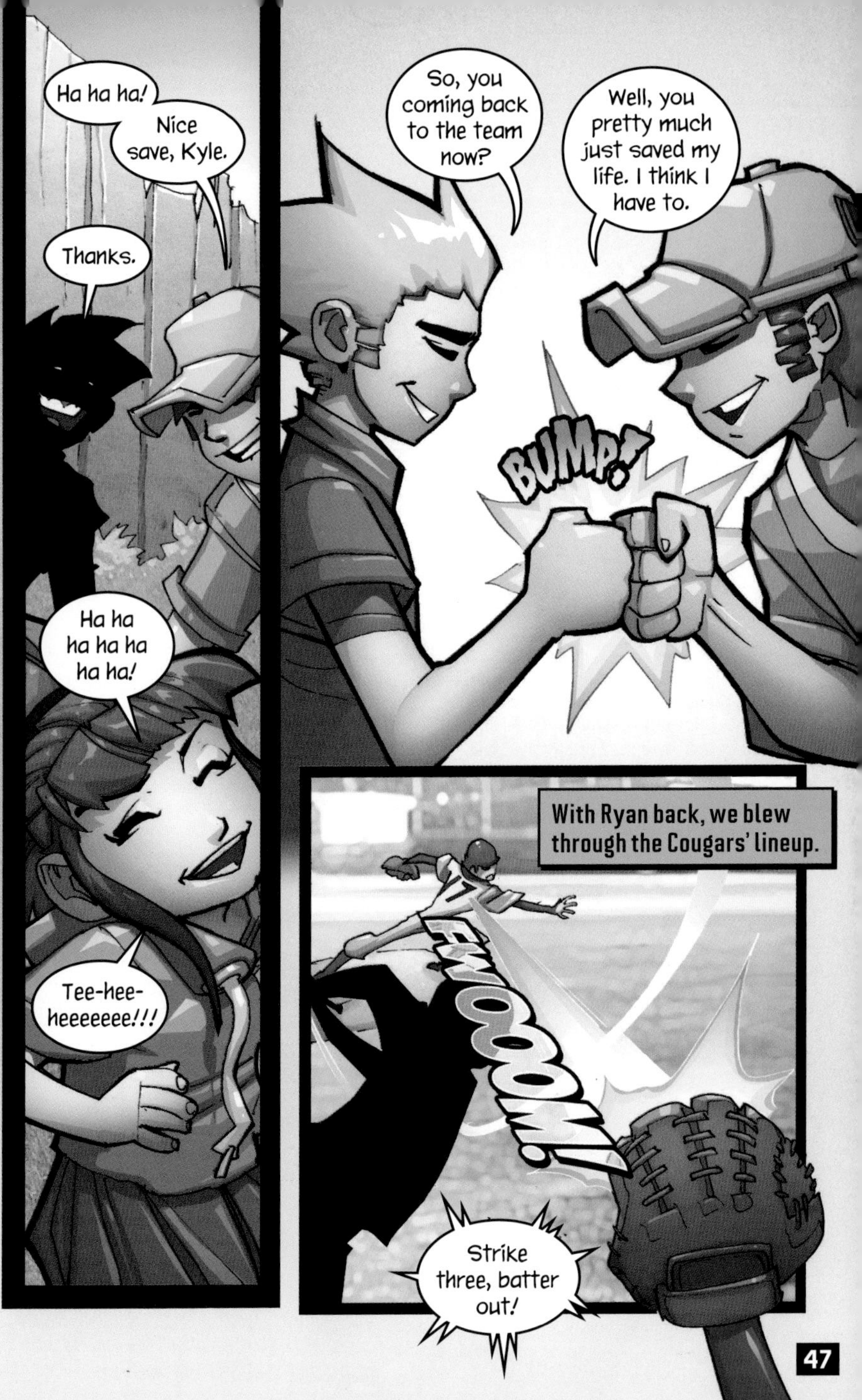

Ha ha ha!
Nice save, Kyle.
Thanks.
Ha ha ha ha ha ha ha!
Tee-hee-heeeeeee!!!
So, you coming back to the team now?
Well, you pretty much just saved my life. I think I have to.
BUMP!
With Ryan back, we blew through the Cougars' lineup.
FWOOOOM!
Strike three, batter out!

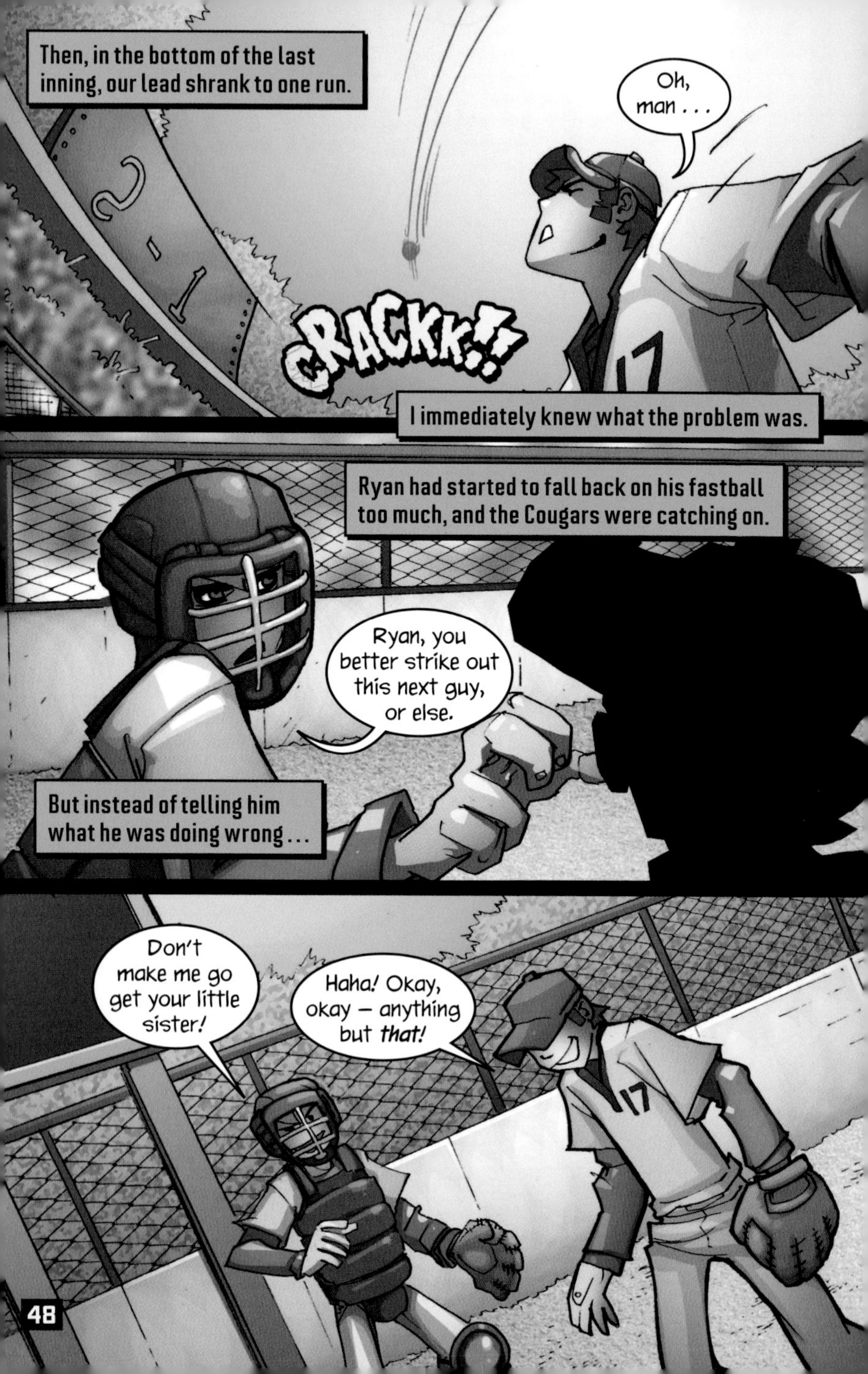

Then, in the bottom of the last inning, our lead shrank to one run.
Oh, man . . .
CRACKK!!
I immediately knew what the problem was.
Ryan had started to fall back on his fastball too much, and the Cougars were catching on.
Ryan, you better strike out this next guy, or else.
But instead of telling him what he was doing wrong . . .
Don't make me go get your little sister!
Haha! Okay, okay — anything but *that!*
17

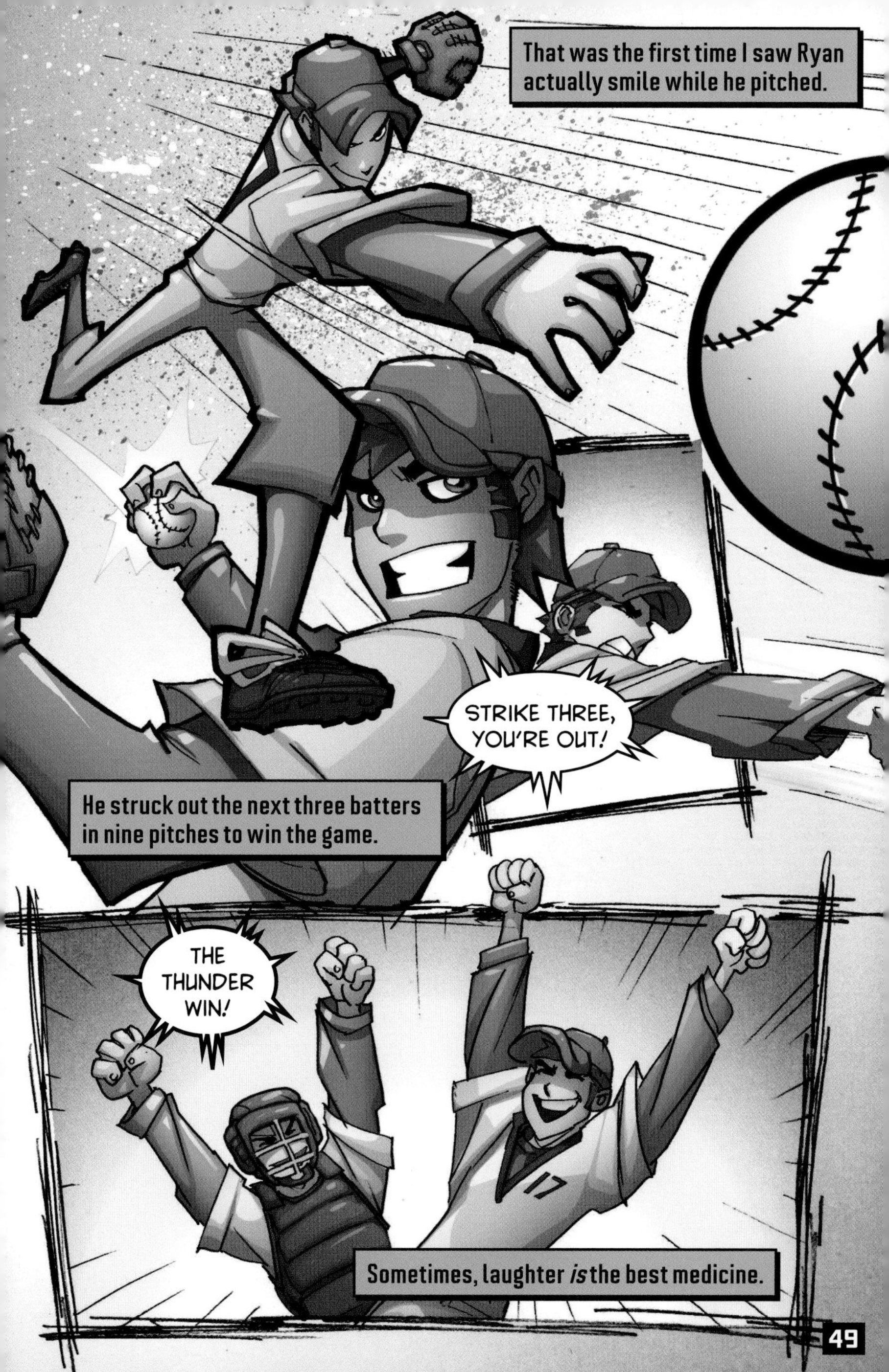
That was the first time I saw Ryan actually smile while he pitched.
STRIKE THREE, YOU'RE OUT!
He struck out the next three batters in nine pitches to win the game.
THE THUNDER WIN!
Sometimes, laughter *is* the best medicine.

# SPORTS ZONE
## POSTGAME RECAP

**BSL**
BASEBALL

**PNT**
PAINTBALL

**FBL**
FOOTBALL

**SOC**
SOCCER

**BBL**
BASKETBALL

# FORMER ENEMIES TEAM UP AND TAKE BACK STATE TITLE!

## BY THE NUMBERS

**FINAL SCORE:**
THUNDER: 4
COUGARS: 3

**STORY:** Whatever their problems were, Kyle Walker and Ryan Rogan were able to overcome them — and they did so just in time to beat the Cougars and take home the state title! When asked how they were able to get along, Kyle just said,"Sometimes you just gotta laugh about stuff and let things sort themselves out."

## Sports Illustrated KIDS

**UP NEXT:** SI KIDS INFO CENTER

# SZ POSTGAME EXTRA

WHERE YOU ANALYZE THE GAME!

BLZ vs BKS 3-1
TGR vs RDR 33-32
EAG vs BAN 14-7
SPA vs WLD 4-3
BAN vs RDR 21-15
RZR vs LIG 4-3
BLZ vs BKS 3-1

Baseball fans got a real treat today when Ryan Rogan and Kyle Walker teamed up to take home the state title. Let's go into the stands and ask some fans for their opinions on the day's big game . . .

## DISCUSSION QUESTION 1

Who was more to blame for their arguments — Kyle or Ryan? Why?

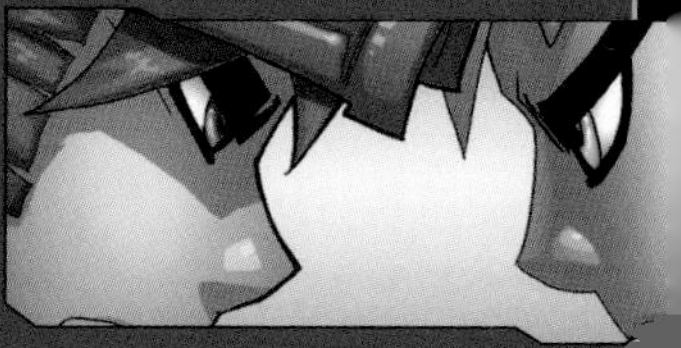

## DISCUSSION QUESTION 2

Ryan is a pitcher and Kyle is a catcher. Which position would you rather play?

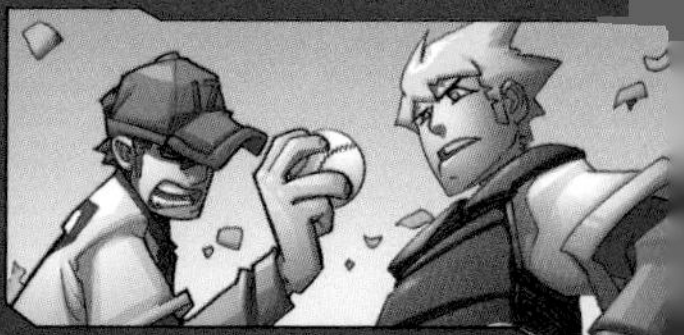

## WRITING PROMPT 1

Ryan was benched a few times. What do you think went through his head when he was forced to leave the game? Write about what Ryan thought.

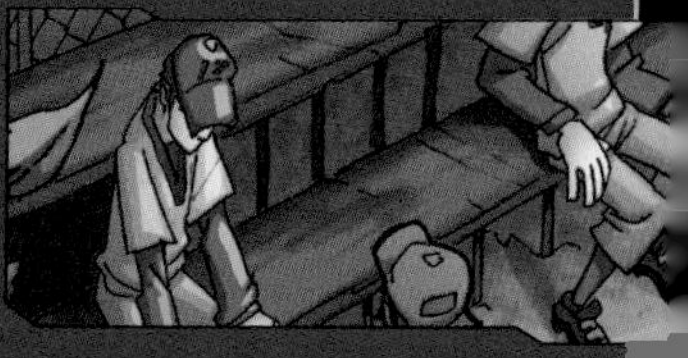

## WRITING PROMPT 2

What is the hardest position to play in baseball? What makes that position difficult? What skills do you have that would make you good at it? Write about your baseball talents.

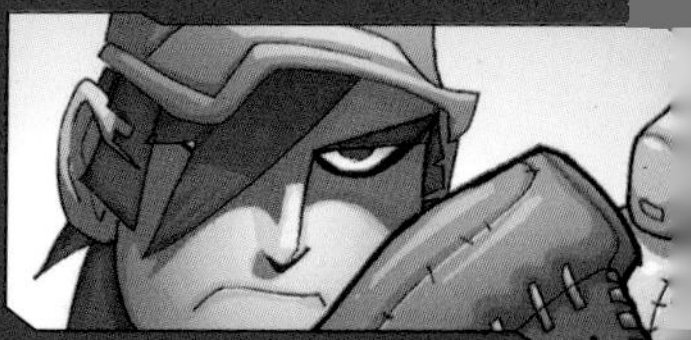

KYLE PICKS RYAN ROGAN TO BE CO-CAPTAIN OF THUND

SIK TICKER

Sports Illustrated KIDS

# INFO CENTER

## GLOSSARY

**ARC** (ARK)—a curved line or path of travel

**CHANGEUP** (CHAYNJ-up)—a slow pitch that is meant to trick the batter into thinking it's a fast pitch

**DISTRACT** (diss-TRAKT)—if someone distracts you, that person weakens your concentration on what you are doing

**PANIC** (PAN-ik)—a sudden feeling of great terror, fright, or worry

**PEP TALK** (PEP TOK)—if you give someone a pep talk, you try to raise their spirits and make them happier or more confident

**PREDICTABLE** (pred-DIKT-uh-buhl)—if you are predictable, then people can guess what you will do next

**SIGNALED** (SIG-nuhld)—gestured or motioned with your hands to someone in order to tell them something, like a pitch call

**TOLERATE** (TOL-ur-rate)—put up with something or someone

**WILD PITCH** (WILDE PICH)—a bad throw by a pitcher that misses the batter's box altogether or hits the batter

# CREATORS

### Eric Fein › Author

Eric Fein is a freelance writer and editor. He has written dozens of comic book stories featuring The Punisher, Spider-Man, Iron Man, Conan, and even Godzilla. He has also written more than forty books and graphic novels for educational publishers. As an editor, Eric has worked on books featuring Spider-Man, Venom, and Batman, as well as several storybooks, coloring and activity books, and how-to-draw books.

### Gerardo Sandoval › Illustrator

Gerardo Sandoval is a professional comic book illustrator from Mexico. He has worked on many well-known comics including Tomb Raider books from Top Cow Production. He has also worked on designs for posters and card sets.

### Benny Fuentes › Colorist

Benny Fuentes lives in Villahermosa, Tabasco in Mexico, where the temperature is just as hot as the sauce is. He studied graphic design in college, but now he works as a full-time colorist in the comic book and graphic novel industry for companies like Marvel, DC Comics, and Top Cow Productions. He shares his home with two crazy cats, Chelo and Kitty, who act like they own the place.

Sports Illustrated KIDS GRAPHIC NOVELS

QUICK COMIC

## JUSTIN JAMES and CARLOS RUIZ IN: BATTLE FOR HOME PLATE

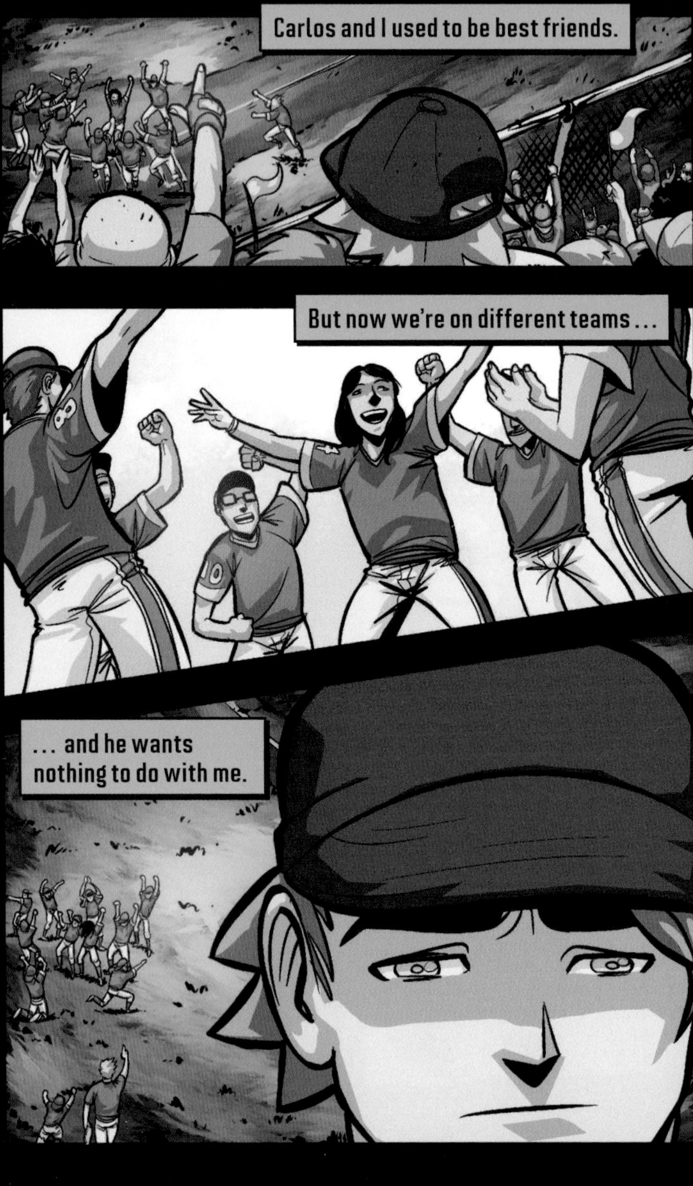

Carlos and I used to be best friends.
But now we're on different teams . . .
. . . and he wants nothing to do with me.


*» LOVE THIS QUICK COMIC? READ THE WHOLE STORY IN BATTLE FOR HOME PLATE – ONLY FROM STONE ARCH BOOKS!*

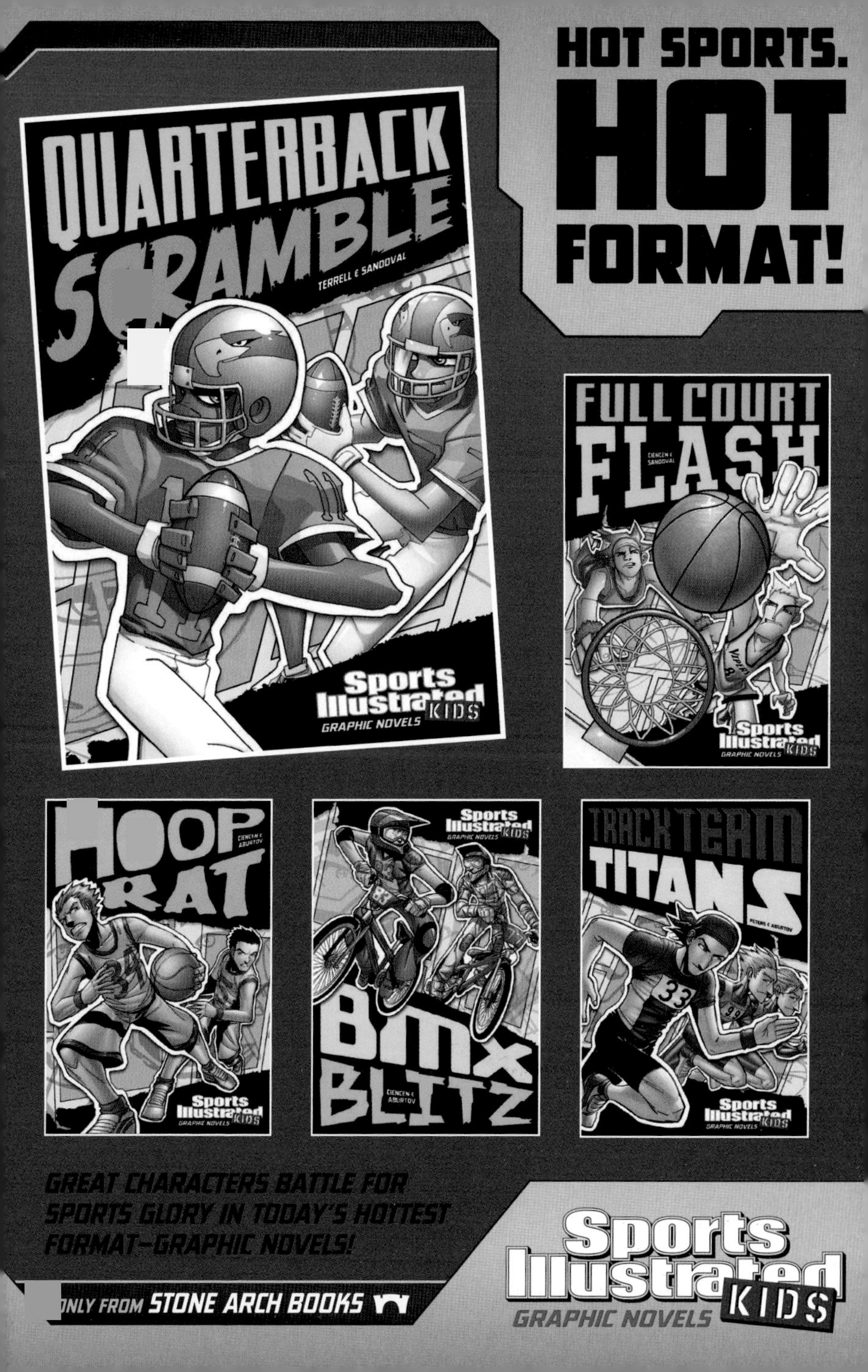
HOT SPORTS.
HOT
FORMAT!
QUARTERBACK SCRAMBLE
TERRELL & SANDOVAL
Sports Illustrated KIDS GRAPHIC NOVELS
FULL COURT FLASH
CIENCIN & SANDOVAL
Sports Illustrated KIDS GRAPHIC NOVELS
HOOP RAT
CIENCIN & ABURTOV
Sports Illustrated KIDS GRAPHIC NOVELS
Sports Illustrated KIDS GRAPHIC NOVELS
BMX BLITZ
CIENCIN & ABURTOV
TRACK TEAM TITANS
PETERS & ABURTOV
Sports Illustrated KIDS GRAPHIC NOVELS
GREAT CHARACTERS BATTLE FOR SPORTS GLORY IN TODAY'S HOTTEST FORMAT—GRAPHIC NOVELS!
ONLY FROM STONE ARCH BOOKS
Sports Illustrated KIDS GRAPHIC NOVELS

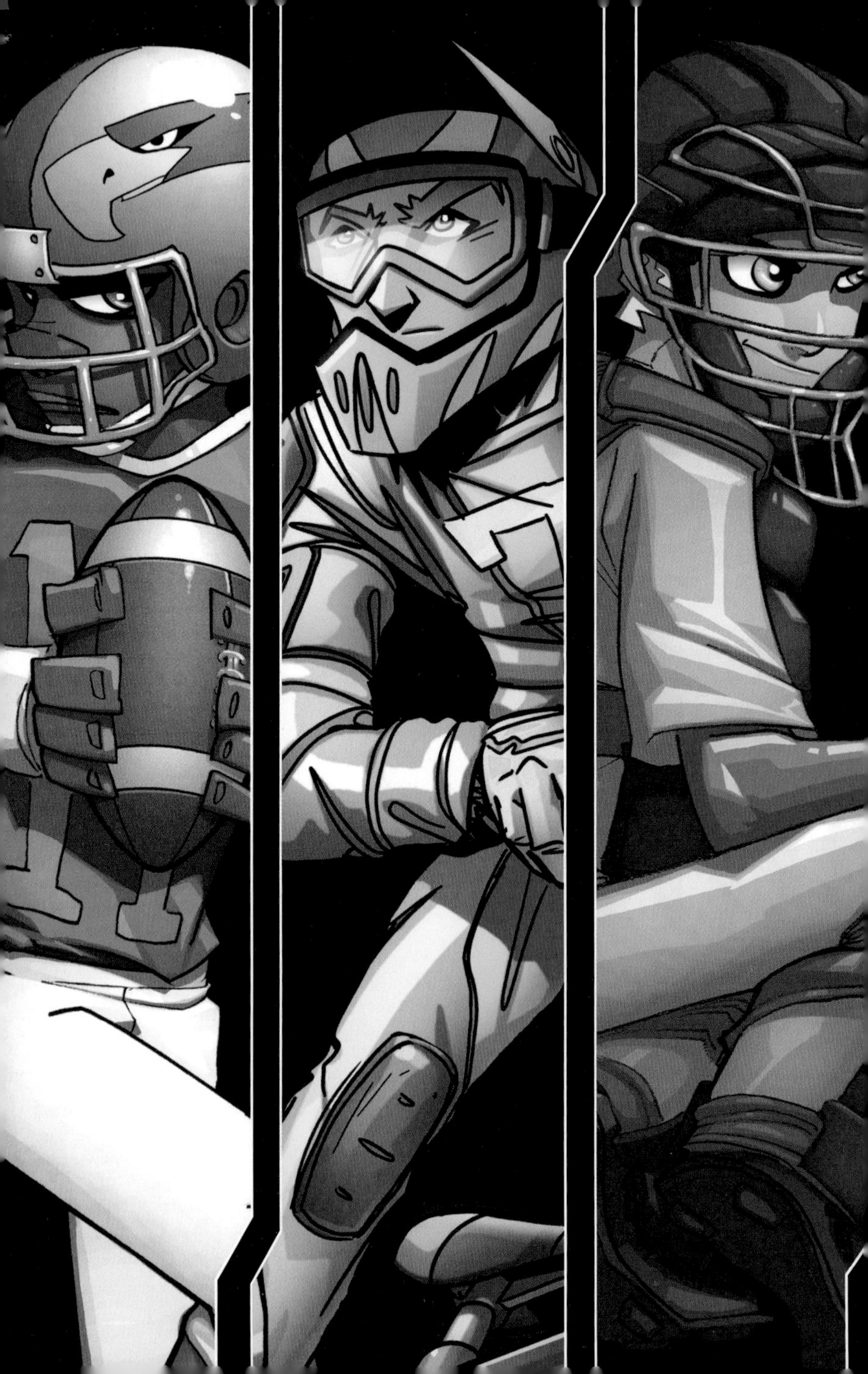

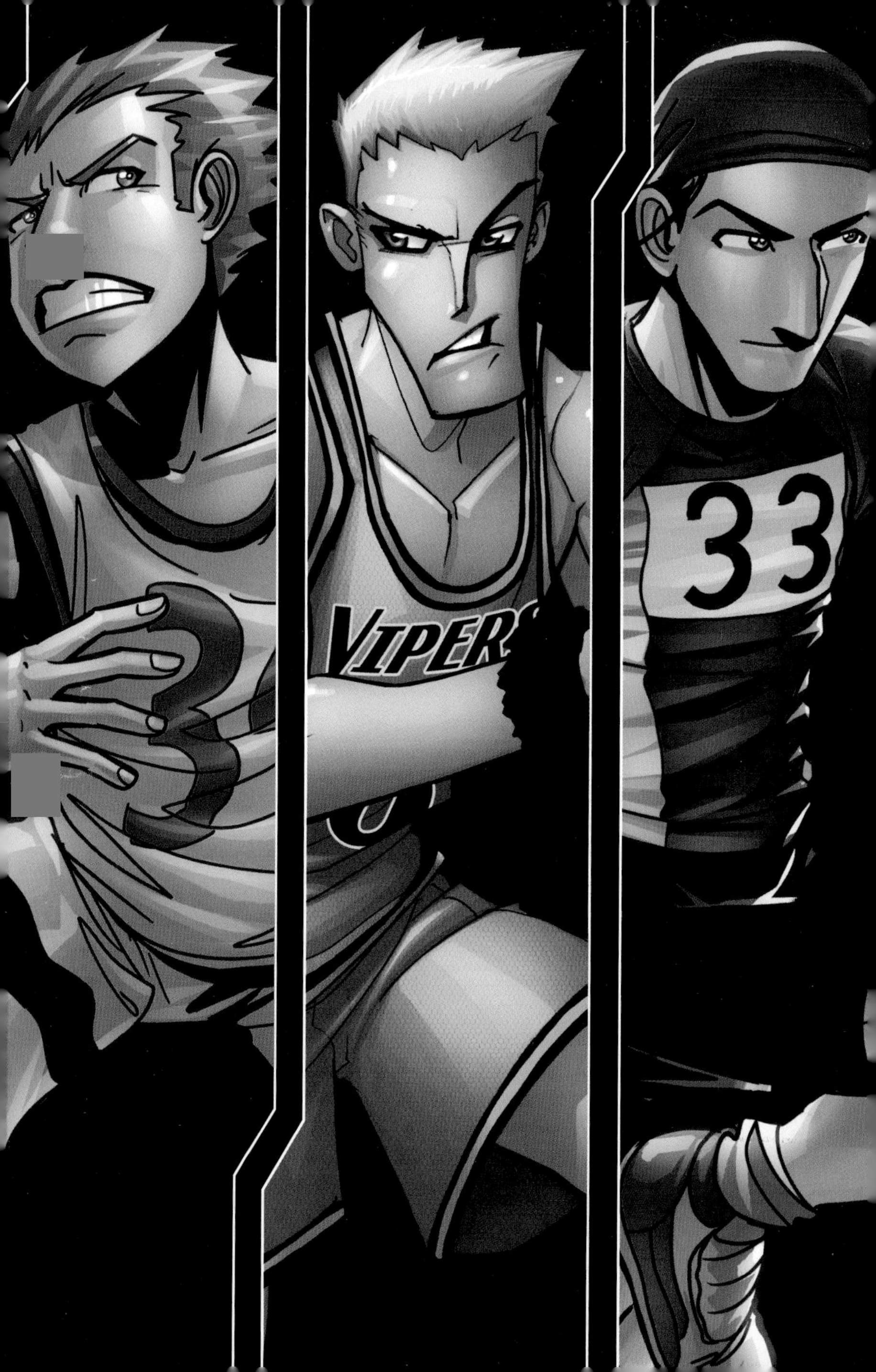
VIPERS
33

Sports Illustrated KIDS

GRAPHIC NOVELS

STONE ARCH BOOKS
a capstone imprint